Gather Ye Rosebuds

Gather Ye Rosebuds

Joan Smith

ROBERT HALE · LONDON

© Joan Smith 1993
First published in Great Britain 2000

ISBN 0 7090 6577 9

Robert Hale Limited
Clerkenwell House
Clerkenwell Green
London EC1R 0HT

2 4 6 8 10 9 7 5 3 1

This edition published by arrangement with
The Ballantine Publishing Group, a division of
Random House Inc.

Typeset by
Derek Doyle & Associates, Liverpool.
Printed in Great Britain by
St Edmundsbury Press Ltd, Bury St Edmunds, Suffolk.
Bound by Woolnough Bookbinding Ltd.

Chapter One

'This will take a deal of work, melady,' Brodagan said, shaking her head in grim anticipation of the job before us. 'An ant itself couldn't find room to perch in this jumbled-up old attic.'

The 'melady' was an honorary title, to remind us that Mrs Brodagan had known better days than working for plain Mrs Barron. In her youth in Ireland, she had peeled potatoes for six months in the kitchen of Dublin House. Her own title of 'Mrs' was assumed as well. Mrs Brodagan had never known marital bliss, for which every bachelor in Christendom should get down on his knees and thank the Almighty.

Brodagan could strike fear into the heart of an Attila. She has shoulders like a horse, and stands five feet ten inches in her stocking feet. Taking into account her towering white headdress, she tops six and a half feet. The headdress of starched linen, similar in construction to a bishop's miter, was assumed at the same time as her title. Before that, she was plain Abigail Brodagan and wore a decent cap. Her dark hair grows blacker with each passing year. It has the unnatural gloss conferred on boots by the application of Kelly's Boot Black. She wears a rustling white apron over her black gowns, and is such a confirmed pessimist that she actually enjoys disaster. She can espy it lurking in the most innocent of events. Mama says (behind her back) that the reason Brodagan will not have her ailing tooth drawn is that she enjoys the pain, but I do not go quite that far. Now that I have denigrated her to my heart's content, I must add that she is also an admirable housekeeper and cook.

Mama and I looked at the jumbled room, which would indeed take a deal of work to transform into my art studio. Until six months before, it had been Uncle Barry's bedroom. Barry McShane was Mama's brother, since deceased. His career was in India, working for 'John Company', otherwise known as the East India Company. With what he called 'the McShane luck', he had returned from gold-paved India empty-handed save for his pension. He came to visit us after a short visit home to Ireland, and never left. For five years he had lived in the east tower wing of our house. He insisted on paying room and board like a regular lodger. Uncle Barry was very little trouble, and it was nice to have a man in the house, as Papa had died the year before.

Now that my uncle was gone, however, I meant to turn his room into my studio. It is a pretty octagonal room looking out over the rolling Kent countryside, liberally sprinkled with fruit trees, wooded hills, and meadowed valleys. With windows on three sides, it gives good light for my painting. It is actually a part of the attic, but with its own staircase, which makes it nice and private. But before I took occupancy, there was 'a deal of work' to be done clearing away the bedroom furniture and Uncle's rubbish.

'You'll not be wanting that bed for a start,' Brodagan informed me, nodding her miter at the bed hung with gold draperies of ancient vintage.

'No, though I shall keep the desk and a couple of chairs, and perhaps the old dresser, to hold my supplies.'

6

The furnishings were the lesser part of the room's contents. Like any traveler in a strange land, my uncle had brought home several trunks of souvenirs. Gaudy shawls hung on chairbacks, an elephant's foot designed as an umbrella stand was full of bric-à-brac. A brass statue of Shiva, a mischievous Indian god with an improbable number of arms, stood on the desk. The clothespress held not only his clothing but more cartons of souvenirs.

'A regular everything shop,' Brodagan declared.

'One hardly knows where to begin,' Mama said, looking about with a vaguely troubled air. Mama always seems to me a creature of yesterday, a delicate Fragonard lady, perhaps. She is small, pale, and pretty. Her copper hair is beginning to soften to grey, but her eyes are still a lustrous blue. She was in mourning for her brother. Six months was considered enough for a mere niece, however. With the arrival of June, I had returned to colored gowns.

'I'll have Steptoe bring up some boxes from the cellar and take this lot to the attics,' Brodagan said, with a sweeping gesture at bed, desk, shawls, elephant's foot, and Shiva.

Mama is one of those ladies who cannot throw anything out. The attic was already jammed from floor to ceiling with the detritus of twenty-six years. She walked to the bed and laid a sentimental hand on its dusty silk curtains. 'These hangings came with me from Ireland, Zoie,' she said. Ireland, you must know, is sacrosanct. If she had brought a piece of peat bog with her, it would still find a place at Hernefield.

'Brodagan will see they are carefully packed away, Mama.'

Mama moved to the desk and picked up a chipped glass inkpot with a silver-plated lid, the silver mostly rubbed away. 'I remember Barry had this inkpot for his sixteenth birthday. He used to speak of being a writer. I shall put it on the desk in the study.'

The desk already had two inkpots, but never mind. The first priority was to get it out of my studio. She toured the room, assigning other worn-out items a place belowstairs. As the octagonal room was at the very top of the house, I knew she would not return often. I would wait until she left before telling Brodagan to have the worn-out carpet and curtains removed, or they would end up in the morning parlour, or saloon.

With a last sighing look around, Mama said, 'I shall send Steptoe up with the boxes, Brodagan. You will remember to set aside the inkpot, and take care with those bed hangings. They are valuable.'

'You run along, melady,' Brodagan said. 'I'll have this jumble cleared away while you'd be saying one, two, three.'

Mama left, and I began to remove Uncle's jackets from the clothespress. 'The press can stay here, Brodagan,' I said. 'It is too heavy to move. It might be useful for storage.'

Brodagan lifted a blue jacket from its hanger and studied it. 'It's many a twist life does,' she said morosely. 'There is Mr Barry, stretched out on his back growing grass, and he not a day older than myself. There was a time he was the most spoken-of man in Wicklow. Oh, the high-and-mighty ladies courted him. His old da tried to set him up with Lord Munster's gal. But there, he preferred an inch of 'want' to a foot of 'should' and darted off to India to escape her. 'Tis a pity he fell amongst thieves,' she said, not without satisfaction.

This last sinister sentence referred to a little misunderstanding with John Company. My uncle was the chief accountant at Calcutta. One of his assistants made off with some company funds, but the culprit was found and most of the money returned. As the man's superior, however, Barry bore a part of the blame, and retired a little earlier than he had intended.

Steptoe, the butler, arrived with the boxes. I left the servants to

8

their chore and went to the blue spare room that I had been using as my studio. I gathered up my paints, brushes, and equipment and put them in an old bandbox for removal to my new studio. It had taken a deal of convincing to get Mama's permission to use the octagonal tower for this purpose. She feared, I think, that I was becoming too serious about my art, and might use it as a substitute for a husband.

She was right to be concerned. I am not one of those ladies who leap at the altar as though it were a throne. I have not yet met the man whom I prefer to a paintbrush. My earliest memories are of holding a pen in my fingers, trying to put on paper what I saw. Dogs, cats, birds, horses, and later, the human face and form. Landscape has little appeal for me. My interest became an obsession shortly after my uncle's arrival from India. Uncle Barry thought my talent was a little out of the ordinary, and encouraged me. He took Mama and myself to Brighton on a holiday, and there I met Count Borsini at an art exhibit. I made bold enough to compliment him on his paintings; mentioned my own difficulty in setting an eye, and before we left Brighton two weeks later, he had been kind enough to call on us and critique my work for me.

It was a delightful surprise to meet him in Aldershot that autumn. He usually spent the winter in London, but he was tired of following his patrons about. As his interest was changing from portraits to landscapes, of which Kent has a plentiful supply, he set up a permanent home-cum-studio at Aldershot. He inquired how my work was progressing; I complained a little at my lack of progress, and before we parted, he had agreed to give me a series of lessons. When he is not too busy (and he is not usually *that* busy), he comes to Hernefield once a week, on Tuesday at two o'clock, instructs me for two hours, has tea, and returns to town.

Barry was usually our chaperon when he was alive. Now that he is gone, the duty has fallen to Mama or Brodagan, or my friend Mrs Chawton. As it is the human form I paint, the chaperon serves double duty as model. On fine days, the lessons take place outdoors. Come autumn, they will move into my studio. The matter of chaperonage has been much discussed. The current plan is to enlarge the class to include a more mature lady to save Mama and Brodagan the stairs. Mrs Chawton, the doctor's wife, is the only one who has showed the least interest thus far, and I fear her interest is more in Borsini than art.

Did I mention he is a monstrously handsome bachelor? He is Italian, of course, with the darkly romantic Latin looks that young English ladies like, and English gentlemen envy. The count is the younger son, with no expectation of inheriting his papa's palazzo in Venice. At least I think it is in Venice, although he once mentioned his papa had sent him wine from his vineyards in Tuscany. Perhaps the Borsinis have more than one estate.

Brodagan used to call him a 'twister', and say he was too 'cute' for me, which was her way of saying he was angling for my poor five-thousand dowry. I was quick to remind her he had painted the Prince Regent, and was not likely to need my pittance. But I think her dislike really softened to adoration when he began honoring her with a burlesque flirtation.

I tidied up the blue room while waiting for Brodagan and Steptoe to clear away my studio. I had dropped a bottle of linseed oil on the carpet of the blue room, which meant some furniture re-arrangement to conceal it. I made a mental note to have Steptoe remove the carpet from Uncle Barry's room. It is impossible to paint in a carpeted room. I would splurge and have matting laid down. I meant to leave the windows uncurtained, have the walls painted a severe white (which Borsini said

10

reflected the light well), and make the room as professional-looking as ten pounds could contrive. A second easel was definitely on my shopping list. Mrs Chawton could use it during the lessons, and in the interim, I could have two paintings going at once. When Uncle Barry and I visited Borsini's studio at Aldershot, he had not less than four easels occupied.

At five-and-twenty, I have ceased thinking of marriage and decided to devote my life to my first love – art. Borsini feels the only reason the world has so few successful lady artists is marriage. Art is a full-time career. How can one devote all her attention to it when she must be worrying about children, meals, and entertaining her husband's colleagues? Borsini has noticed a great improvement in my work. My palette, he said, was too light. His own sparkles with the jewel tones of ruby, emerald, sapphire, and topaz, but somehow I cannot find these rich hues in the human face.

With time to spare, I began a sketch. The quantity of self-portraits in my collection does not denote self-love, but a shortage of models. When I am alone, I often sit in front of the mirror and sketch myself, as Rembrandt did. The hand must be trained to do what the artist wants, and like any other craft, practice makes perfect. I pulled the chair close to the mirror, propped my sketchpad on my knee, and studied the familiar face in the mirror.

I doubt there are many ladies who are as familiar with the lineaments of their face as I. Borsini is kind enough to tell me I have a classical face, which is not quite accurate. He has that easy Latin way with a compliment. My face is the proper Grecian shape, however, and my green eyes well spaced. I have lately taken to arranging my black hair in a Grecian knot, more for convenience than to ape the Greeks. It is really the nose that falls considerably short of the classical ideal – or perhaps I should say, falls long. Venus had not such a long nose, nor such wide lips. My mentor tells me it is the straying from the ideal that confers that peculiar uniqueness of true perfection. I know well enough that 'perfection' does not encompass such a far straying from the ideal as my own features. I have been called pretty, never beautiful – except by Borsini.

Time has a way of flying by when I am at work. I was vaguely aware of boxes being carried down from the octagonal tower, along the hall, and up the other staircase to the attic. When Brodagan's towered head appeared at the door, she said, 'It's teatime, melady. Your studio is cleared away, if ye'd care to cast a glance at it. I'll not drag my poor old legs up them stairs again. Seven trips, it took. I don't know how in the world I did it. You have the youth still. You can take a run up.'

'Thank you, Brodagan,' I said, and set aside my sketch to dart up the narrow staircase. Brodagan is not much interested in her salary, but she is greedy for praise.

Steptoe was still there, just opening the dresser drawers. Our butler is our only English servant. Mama brought servants with her from the old country when she married, and has replaced them with other Irish servants as they retired or passed away. Steptoe has a polite contempt for all of them except Brodagan, whom he fears. He is of middle years and medium stature, with brown hair just turning grey. I can scarcely write his name without adding Brodagan's favorite adjective for him, 'uppity'. Steptoe was used to work for the local nobility, Lady Weylin.

'Shall I clear away your late uncle's linens, madam?' he asked. Steptoe always called both Mama and myself 'madam'.

'Yes, put all his clothing in boxes. I shall have it taken to the poorhouse.' Even Mama would not insist on keeping old clothing.

He began lifting shirts from the top drawer while I strolled around the room, seeing it in my mind's eye with the bed gone, the curtains down, the floor covered in matting, and the walls painted a bright, reflecting white. When I turned back to Steptoe, he was holding a small leather bag, dangling from his fingers by a cord.

'What is that, Steptoe?' I asked.

He handed it to me. 'It rattles, madam,' he said.

I loosened the string and shook the contents out into my palm. The sunbeam slanting through the windows caught the object in my palm and reflected a myriad of iridescent rainbows. A muted gasp hung on the air as I gazed in disbelief at the object. I searched for the clasp and held it to catch the sun's full beams. It was a beautiful diamond necklace. From a chain of smallish diamonds, a large sunburst of larger stones suspended at the front. I am not familiar with the terminology of diamond cutting, but I could see there were various shapes and cuts of stones in the sunburst, some of the stones quite large.

Uncle Barry had no fortune. He paid his board from his company pension. 'Where on earth did he get this?' I asked. For a wonderful sixty seconds I thought uncle had made his fortune in India after all. Some prince had given him the diamonds as a reward for saving his life. Uncle told many such wonderful tales. The nawabs, it seemed, had no notion of the value of gems. In that sixty seconds I had set out on a tour of Italy to study the masters, with Borsini as my guide. Mama and I would hire an Italian villa, and visit Florence, the birthplace of the Renaissance. We would float in a gondola down the Grand Canal in Venice to the Palazzo Borsini.

Steptoe came and peered closely over my shoulder. He cleared his throat and said, with a sly look, 'It looks very much like the necklace Lady Margaret MacIntosh reported stolen five years ago, madam.'

13

'Stolen! Good God! You mean to say Uncle Barry was a thief!'

'That would not be for me to say, madam, but it is certainly the same necklace, or one exactly like it.'

Chapter Two

I ran downstairs as fast as my legs could carry me, to find Mama waiting impatiently at the tea table. She lifted the pot and began pouring as soon as she saw me. I ran, gasping, and held the necklace out for her to see.

She blinked in confusion. 'What is that, Zoie? Where did you get it? Why, it looks like – *diamonds!*'

'It is. Steptoe says it is Lady Margaret MacIntosh's stolen necklace.'

Mama's fingers flew to her lips to stifle a gasp. She looked around, to see no spies were listening. 'Where did it come from?' She drew back against the sofa cushions, refusing to touch it.

'It was hidden in Uncle Barry's dresser. He was a thief, Mama! What shall we do with this?'

'Are you sure it is hers?'

'Steptoe says it is. You have a look at it.'

She steeled herself to touch it then. She turned it this way and that in her fingers, with a troubled frown. 'I fear he is right. Steptoe would know. Butlers always know everything. And you recall he worked as head footman at Parham for several years. He would have seen it any number of times.'

15

Parham is the estate of our neighbor, Lord Weylin. When he is not at London, he lives there with his widowed mama, a social whale amidst the minnows of the area. Until Lady Margaret's death a year ago, she also lived at Parham to keep her sister, Lady Weylin, company.

Five years ago, Lady Margaret's diamond necklace was stolen. As its loss coincided with my uncle's arrival at Hernefield, it began to look as though Uncle was nothing else but a thief.

'I wonder if Barry made a habit of this sort of thing,' Mama said fearfully. 'I mean to say, it is odd that he should steal just this one necklace.'

'Don't say such things, Mama!' I exclaimed, and sank to the sofa. As soon as I caught my breath, I saw she was right. I was mortally afraid to return to the tower and look in other drawers, but if Uncle Barry was a thief, it was best to know the worst. 'I shall go upstairs and search.'

Mama had drawn out a handkerchief and was fanning herself, as befitted a Fragonard lady. 'I shall stay here and catch my breath. Oh dear, whatever shall we do? You know I never had but a waxen head, Zoie. You must decide what is to be done.'

I gave her hand a reassuring pat and darted back up the two flights of stairs to the octagonal tower. Steptoe had been seized with the same idea as Mama and myself. He had opened all the drawers of both dresser and desk and rooted through them. They stood open and disarranged.

'There does not appear to be any further booty, madam,' he said, relishing that offensive 'booty'.

'Keep looking. All his jackets and boots – everything will have to be searched. Let me know if you find anything.'

'Yes, madam.'

His snuff-brown eyes were full of sated spite. He could hardly hold his lips steady as he began unfolding socks and smallclothes, shaking them out. When we were finished, I returned to Mama and told her no more booty had been discovered.

'Thank goodness. What shall we do with that?' she asked, pointing to the necklace as if it were a dead rat. She had placed it on the far end of the sofa table. 'Lady Margaret is dead and gone. Perhaps if we just hid it away in the attic—'

'Mama! That is no solution. We must return it to Parham, and let them decide what is to be done with it.'

'Lady Weylin has enough diamonds. She will never miss it.'

'It may belong to Lady Margaret's stepson – entailed, is what I mean. We cannot keep it. That is dishonest.'

'Oh my dear woe! The shame of it. Is there no way we could smuggle it into Parham without saying where it has been all this while? Through the mail, perhaps . . .'

'Trust diamonds to the mail? That is risky.'

'And someone might see us mailing it, too. We could call on Lady Weylin, and slide it down the back of a sofa, or into a vase. It would be found eventually, and they need not know Barry stole it.'

'We are never invited to Parham, Mama,' I reminded her.

One did not drop in uninvited on the Weylins. They held themselves very high. I had been there exactly three times in my twenty-five years, always with a crowd. Lord Weylin became friendly at election time, and held a large, raucous party. Unfortunately, there was no election in the offing.

'You don't think Lady Weylin might like to share your lessons with Borsini?' Mama asked. 'You could stop by and ask her. He is a count, after all; she is only a countess.'

I liked to think Borsini was a count, but in fact, I did not really believe it. It was only a pleasant fiction. The image of stately Lady Weylin climbing up two flights of stairs to my little studio was too ludicrous to contemplate without smiling. 'No, that will not fadge.'

'What of that Book Society you are working up?'

The Book Society was Mrs Chawton's project. She had read of some book-loving ladies banding together, each contributing a certain sum to buy a book, which they all read and discussed.

'Is Lady Weylin bookish?' I asked.

'I see her at the circulating library from time to time. That suggests she is, and also that she is not fond of laying down her gold to buy the book herself. I think we must tackle it, Zoie. It is that or confessing that Barry was a thief. And at the worst possible time. The Season just closed last week; Lord Weylin is home for a visit. Perhaps Mrs Chawton would like to go with you?'

I could not think the Weylins would appreciate a social call from the doctor's wife, whose brother runs the taproom. The Chawtons barely pass for quality in Aldershot. Mama and I would hardly be welcome, but at least we were an old, genteel family.

'There is no weaseling out of it, Mama. You must come with me. You try to distract Lady Weylin for a moment, and I shall pop the necklace into a vase, or down the side of the sofa.'

'Let us do it tomorrow, Zoie. I shall need the evening to worry about it.'

'It will be best to make sure Barry has no more secrets hidden away before we go. If Steptoe unearths more booty, we must find some other way to return it.'

'I cannot believe it of Barry,' Mama said, idly sipping her tea. 'I know it troubled him that he came home so poor, when half of his colleagues were nabobs, but it is not as though he actually needed the money. I mean to say he did not sell the necklace, but just hid it away. It is so very odd. Could he have been one of those kleptomaniacs like Mrs Flanagan, who took the bolt of ribbon from the drapery shop?'

'What I wonder is how he ever got next or nigh the necklace. He was never at Parham, was he?'

'Why no, he was not,' Mama said, brightening. 'He was in London when Weylin had his last election do. And really, you know, I seem to remember Lady Margaret lost it at Tunbridge Wells. She used to go there often for the chalybeate waters.'

'Uncle Barry never went to Tunbridge Wells, as far as I can remember.'

'No, why would he? He was healthy as a horse – until he died, I mean. He was used to run up to London as often as he could find an excuse. He liked to visit at East India House, and chat to the lads, but Tunbridge Wells – never.'

'So how did he get the necklace?' I asked.

Mama bent her mind to this problem and soon came up with an answer. 'This goes from bad to worse, Zoie. He must have been part of a gang! One of them did the robbing, and others peddled the goods.'

'If that were the case, he should have been rich. You know he hadn't a sou to his name when he died. One would have thought he would have squirreled away a couple of hundred pounds at least. He had no expensive habits.'

'And I only took a nominal sum from him for board,' Mama added. 'Why, from his pension alone he ought to have saved up a few hundred. I made sure his savings would at least bury him, but I had to pay for the coffin along with everything else. He must have been a secret gambler,' she decided, as she could think of nothing else to explain the mystery.

'Perhaps he had a woman in London,' I suggested. There had been a certain Surinda Joshi in Calcutta. Barry never mentioned her in his letters, but Mama's family used to write about her. They feared he would marry this dusky beauty.

'Now, that is entirely possible. He was always a mouthful among the parish for his flirting ways. He could have been sending money to Surinda.'

19

'It is odd he had not sold the necklace, if that was his plan. The thing was stolen five years ago, and he still had it when he died.'

I never thought I would come to hate the sight of diamonds, but that glittering little heap on the table was enough to make my blood run cold.

Steptoe came in and said, in his uppity way, 'There does not appear to be any more stolen jewels among Mr McShane's belongings, madam. Shall I send the necklace back to Parham?'

'You must not think of it, Steptoe!' Mama exclaimed.

In our confusion, we had forgotten we had Steptoe to contend with. It seemed best to take the bull by the horns. I said, 'We plan to return it secretly, Steptoe. We would appreciate it if you did not speak to the servants, nor indeed to anyone, of the necklace.'

Steptoe remained silent a moment, scanning this for opportunities of exploiting us. He was a perfectly self-centred man. He presented a good appearance and lent a certain cachet when he answered the door, looking down on all our callers, but really he was not at all pleasant.

'Very well, madam. Ah, and while I have your attention, might I inquire whether you have given any thought to the matter of increasing my wage?' he asked, while peering at us from under his lashes.

Steptoe is always after an increase in his wage. He has had three while Brodagan has had one. This latest demand was nothing less than extortion, but it was not the time to chastise him.

'How much increase will you need, Steptoe?' Mama asked fearfully.

'Five pounds per quarter would be convenient, madam.'

'You only asked for three last week!' I objected.

'Yes, madam, but now I find five would be more convenient.' His eyes slid to the diamonds, then turned to Mama with a speaking look. 'Thank you, madam.' He bowed and left.

'That one will be no stranger in hell,' Mama said.

'This is intolerable! We shall not give him another sou.'

'The alternative is to tell Lady Weylin – and Lord Weylin – the truth, Zoie,' she pointed out.

'I daresay we can eke out another five pounds per quarter, but if he demands one more penny, Mama, we must turn him off. Let him tell what stories he likes; no one will listen. People know we are honest.'

'They do not know Barry was honest. There were a few rumors in town about that unfortunate bookkeeping error in India. How very disagreeable it will be, having to call at Parham tomorrow,' Mama said, gazing forlornly into her teacup. 'My blood shakes to think of it, for I haven't the heart of a mouse.'

'We must go in the morning. Borsini will be coming in the afternoon.'

'Gracious, as if having a thief in the family were not bad enough! I hope Weylin is not there when we call. His mama is enough to frighten the dragoons, but if I have to face him with stolen diamonds in my pocket I know I shall drop right out into a confession and land in the roundhouse.'

'Dangle from a gibbet is more like it.'

'Do not say such things, Zoie!' She daubed at her eyes. 'One dislikes to speak ill of the dead, but I do think this was not very nice of Barry, and after I was kind enough to give him a home, too. He did it black on us, Zoie, and that's the truth.' Mama slips into the old Irish expressions when she is upset.

'It is pretty clear that Uncle Barry was pulling the wool over our eyes for years. I have no reluctance to speak ill of him. I always thought he was sly. It would not surprise me if he had his fingers in the till in India.'

'Now, that is not true. They caught the fellow who did it. Barry left the company with a clean record and a full pension.'

'Perhaps, but do you not remember how he used to keep a very sharp eye on the post? He'd be waiting for the delivery, and snatch up his letters, slipping them inside his jacket before anyone got a look at them. They were orders from his gang, I expect.'

'I always thought they were from Surinda. There was a strong musky scent in the hall after he took the letters away. He certainly had something to hide. And with all his treachery, he did not end up rich,' Mama said, 'but left me to pay for his coffin.'

Chapter Three

Once Steptoe learned our secret, the only person in the house with any vestige of control over him was Brodagan. He was becoming bossy even with her, which brought her to the saloon to complain. We took her into our confidence regarding the necklace and asked for her forbearance at this time. She was marble-constant, as usual. Brodagan would not complain if we murdered the archbishop.

'You may be sure as soon as the matter is straightened out, he will be dismissed,' Mama promised.

'My sorrow!' she declared, black eyes gleaming fiercely. 'A viper in our own bosom. Him in his grand black suit, looking like his nose would bleed if you said boo to him. He's no better than a thief hisself, squeezing money out of a widow. He wants the good wine brought up to his cubbyhole, if you please. I'd sooner part with my eyes than let him have Mr Barron's good claret.'

'Since Mr Barron no longer has need of it . . .' Mama said.

'That old rack-pot is to have ambrosia then, while the rest of us belowstairs make do with small beer?' Brodagan asked, with a gimlet glance that would cut forged steel.

'I think Brodagan would like a bottle of the claret, Mama,' I said, as Mama was not quick to take her meaning.

'You do not have to ask, my dear Brodagan,' Mama said, and won a smile from the Turk. 'Naturally you must do as you wish.'

Having won her point, Brodagan said piously, 'I never touch a drop, melady!' She continued, 'That scarecrow has had the spite in his nose for us ever since he came here, only because we lack a handle to our names. "His lordship did it this way," says he, and "Her ladyship did it that way," as if he was quoting the Bible. Why did he leave Parham and go to the Pakenhams? That is what *I* would like to know. And within a year or two, he hopped along to us. Sure it was a dark day when you hired the likes of that grasshopper, melady.'

'So it was, Brodagan,' Mama agreed, 'but he looked well, you know, and had worked at Parham.'

'If you call sitting on your haunches, swilling wine, work,' Brodagan said. 'I, with my bad tooth roaring like a lion in my mouth, still have the laundry to get folded, and the bread to knead, and my own apron which I pay for myself to iron before this head sees the pillow.'

'Could Mary not—'

'Mary O'Rourke is as much help as a bucket with a hole in it, even if she is my own niece,' she said, and left. Brodagan always got the last word.

Over breakfast the next morning, Mama and I discussed our attack on Parham. As I was to broach the Book Society plan to Lady Weylin, I would be doing most of the talking. When I suggested that Mama slip the diamonds into some convenient hiding place, however, she turned as white as milk and said she really did not think she could. She was bound to drop them, and Lady Weylin would think she had stolen them. She did undertake to distract Lady Weylin for a few moments with some talk of roses, however, while I did the deed.

24

At ten-thirty we set out for Parham in the carriage. Our meadow abuts theirs. It would be only a quarter of an hour's walk across the park, but as we required the dignity of a carriage to call on a countess, we went by the road, a distance of two miles. To enter the wrought-iron gates, guarded by a pair of snarling griffins, was already enough to shatter one's confidence. The closer we drew to the house, the larger and more impressive it grew. Parham was built in the days when homes were fortresses. A tall tower rises high on either end of the façade, with a crenellated roofline holding them together. Although the house has been updated over the centuries, the front still has a forbidding aspect.

'I feel we ought to have brought cannons,' Mama said.

We were not met with guns, but by a butler whose manner made Steptoe look like a friendly pup. Never have I seen eyebrows rise so high, nor heard such arrogance in a servant's tone.

'You wish to speak to her ladyship?' he exclaimed, as if we had said we wished to shoot her.

'If she is not too busy,' Mama said apologetically.

I refused to be browbeaten by a servant. 'It will only take a moment,' I said, and lightly elbowed him aside to walk in. Mama darted in after me.

We were familiar with the grandiosity of the entrance from our few other visits at election time. There was a deal of marble, of exotic carved panelling, of paintings and busted Grecian statuary. Of more interest, there was a doorway leading to the Blue Saloon, where her ladyship sat, thumbing idly through a magazine, with a pug dog at her feet. The butler shunted us into an inferior small parlour used for tradesmen, and said he would inquire whether her ladyship was at home.

'Try the Blue Saloon,' I suggested.

For ten minutes Mama and I waited. We discussed hiding the diamonds in that parlour, but decided against it.

'They might suspect us,' she whispered. 'It will be best to leave it in a room Lady Margaret used.'

'If she refuses to see us, I shall stuff them down the side of this settee before I rise.'

Eventually the butler came and said, 'Her ladyship can spare you a moment now.'

We rose and followed him into the Blue Saloon. It was a regular furniture display room, holding every grand thing you can think of. Persian carpets, brocade window hangings, a plethora of carved mahogany, and a positive glut of bibelots.

Lady Weylin reclined at her ease on a striped satin settee. She looked up from petting her ugly little tan pug and said querulously, 'It is the Barrons, is it not?' We had been neighbors forever. We admitted to being ourselves and advanced into the holy of holies.

It has often been remarked that people resemble their pets, and it was certainly true in this case. Lady Weylin had a broad, short face with widely spaced eyes, a pug nose, and a wrinkled forehead. She had fallen into a sluggish tan complexion and an excess of flesh from lack of exercise. Her toilette, a fashionable gown of wheat-colored lutestring with a lace shawl, was unexceptionable.

She lifted the pug from her lap onto the sofa beside her and waved a hand toward two hard-backed chairs. These offered no likely hiding place, but we sat down.

'What can I do for you?' she asked, very much the grande dame.

Mama was completely capsized by her manner. I braced myself to be ingratiating and said, 'We are setting up a Book Society, Lady Weylin, and wondered if you would be interested.'

'Who is "we"? You and your mama?'

'Myself, and some ladies from Aldershot,' I replied.

'Ah, Aldershot,' she said, as if it were a leper colony. 'And what, pray, is a Book Society?'

I swallowed the urge to ask whether she was not familiar with a book and explained Mrs Chawton's plan – the dues to buy books, the reading by each member, and eventual discussion.

When I had finished, she cocked her head to one side and said, 'Rubbish! You will only put the circulating library out of business. If you and your friends, Miss Barron, have time and money to squander, you might better devote them to charitable works. Reading novels is harmful to girls. It puts ideas in their heads.'

'Surely that is the proper place for them, ma'am.' I felt a sharp kick at my ankle from Mama.

'Not in ladies' heads. If you had been employing your time more usefully, you would not still be single at your age. You would have better things to do than reading books.'

Having met with not only an outright refusal but an insult as well, I was left with nothing to say, and directed a look to Mama. It was difficult to leap straightway into discussing roses, which was the only thing Mama felt capable of discussing. To pave the way, I said, 'What charitable works did you have in mind, ma'am?'

'Helping the poor, of course. That is what charity is – helping the less fortunate.'

This was hardly news to me, but I plodded on, while my eyes skimmed the room for a vase or vessel to hold the booty. 'Lord Weylin is active with the orphans' school, I believe.'

'Yes. Weylin is home – but of course, you knew that.'

Her tone suggested that was why I, the old unmarried one, had come – to try my hand at attaching him. I resented her barbs, but could not dwell on them. My eye alit on a small blue and white Chinese vase on a table near the doorway. We had one like it in the blue guest room at home. Lady Weylin would certainly not bestir herself to accompany us to the door, but I would be directly in her line of sight. Dare I risk it? 'Yes indeed. I had heard he was home,' I said.

'Weylin would not be interested in your Book Society.'

'We had not planned to ask him, ma'am.' Her manner was so brusque that I wanted to escape at once. I would risk the Chinese vase. 'I shall tell the ladies you are not interested, then,' I said, gathering up my gloves and reticule. Mama did likewise, looking a question at me.

The pug opened its mouth to give a desultory yap. Lady Weylin began patting it and talking baby talk. 'Does Bubbums want to go into the garden? Good doggy.' Then she turned to me and said in a less friendly tone than that used with her dog, 'You may tell Seeton on your way out to come for Bubbums.'

I willed down the automatic 'thank you' that rose up at being given permission to do her errand. What I should have done was tell her to call Seeton herself. I rose with a chilly nod and said, 'Mama, are you ready to go now? We have taken enough of Lady Weylin's valuable time.' I allowed my eyes to glare at Bubbums. Mama was more than eager to escape.

'Good day, Lady Weylin,' she said.

Lady Weylin nodded but did not bestir herself to reply. We began pacing the considerable distance to the door, while she resumed the more agreeable conversation with her pug. I pointed to the Chinese pot and whispered, 'I shall drop the necklace in there. You fall a step behind me and cover my back in case she looks.' I slid my hand into my pocket and palmed the diamonds.

I had to walk a step to the right to make the drop. With Mama concealing me as best she could, I reached for the vase. My closed hand was just above it when Mama hissed in my ear. I looked up and saw Lord Weylin hovering at the doorway, not two yards from me.

He has a finely carved face, as sharp and thin as a steel sword. His lean body was stiff with pride. A sleek cap of caramel-colored hair gleamed in the light. A pair of black eyebrows were drawn together in a frown. From beneath them, his stormy grey eyes stared at me as if I were a thief or a murderess. He stepped into the Blue Saloon.

'Are you interested in Chinese porcelain?' he asked, in a voice that implied, *Were you planning to pocket it, miss*?

A flood of heat rose to my face, staining it scarlet. 'Just an admirer,' I managed to get out. 'We have got a little jug just like this at home.'

His long fingers reached possessively and lifted the vase beyond my reach. It was about eight inches high, and of a curious flat shape, decorated with a dragon and scrolled pattern. 'Indeed? I am amazed, for I was given to understand that mine was unique.'

'Ours is a little larger, I believe,' I said, for I wanted to outdo him in something.

'The forgers often make such mistakes, for they do not have the original to work from, but only a picture. What you have, if I am not mistaken, is one of the Italian forgeries from the last century. This original is from the Ming dynasty, circa 1500. It was during the Yuan dynasty that white translucent porcelain with the blue underglaze was first used. This style reached its peak during the Ming period.' His long fingers caressed the vase lovingly as he spoke.

I said, quite at random, 'Very nice.'

'And very valuable,' he added, carefully returning it to its table. 'You ladies are leaving?' His snakelike gaze turned to include Mama in the question.

'We are just on our way out, milord,' she said.

He did not ask why we had come, but those raised eyebrows told me he was wondering, and I mentioned the Book Society. 'Your mama was not interested,' I said.

'We shan't send you off empty-handed, miss . . .' Perhaps the raised eyebrows indicated an uncertainty as to our identity. 'Miss Barron,' he said, apparently recognizing us. 'We have all sorts of books no one reads. I shall have some sent to Hernefield for you ladies to enjoy.'

We had not come hat in hand, begging, but I was so eager to get away that I said, 'Thank you,' in a choked tone, and lunged for the doorway, with Mama scampering behind me.

As we left, I heard Lady Weylin complain loudly, 'I asked her to send Seeton in. Really, the chit has no manners.'

Seeton condescended to get the door for us. 'Her ladyship would like to see you, Seeton,' I said, and left with what dignity I could.

'How horrid!' Mama exclaimed, when we were safely out the door. 'I never felt so unwelcome in my life. She had the tea tray right beside her, and did not even offer us a cup. Rag-mannered, I call it.' I had not noticed the tea tray. 'I don't suppose you managed to drop the diamonds?'

'No, Lord Weylin came too soon. He thinks I was trying to steal that ugly old vase. Did you see the way he glared at me?'

'All the Weylins are excessively toplofty. I felt as welcome as the pox, and the worst of it is, we shall have to come back tomorrow.'

'Not I!' The image of Lord Weylin's haughty form rose up in my mind. He was elegantly tall and thin, but with the broad chest and shoulders of the sportsman. That sleekly barbered hair and those disturbingly dark grey eyes would cause a blush for days to come. His proud, sculpted nose and arrogant chin, the lips drawn in a pinched smile, sent a shiver of shame through me.

'I shall never darken their door again. I would rather be arrested for holding stolen goods.'

'Well I would not! You must come back, Zoie.'

Chapter Four

Mama had a suspiciously convenient attack of rheumatism in her knees that evening. I set out alone for Parham the next morning, again at ten-thirty, as that hour had found her ladyship at home the day before. It was either return the necklace or lock Steptoe in the cellar until we came up with some other plan. He had become so uppity that the matter had to be settled without delay. Once the necklace was back where it belonged, we would send him packing. Let him holler that the diamonds had been found at Hernefield. It was his word against ours, and Brodagan announced that she, for one, was ready to perjure herself in the matter, for she could not draw breath under the same roof as Master Cock o' the Ashes. The good Lord would not demand it of her.

Mama and I felt that once the Weylins had the diamonds, there would be no legal action taken, even if Steptoe told them of our involvement. Lady Weylin was too lethargic to enjoy going to court, and Weylin would not be eager to alienate an old family like ours, with political connections in the parish.

Lord Weylin had, as promised, sent some dusty old books to Hernefield the afternoon before. There was a preponderance of sermons and reformation tracts by such lively writers as John

32

Donne and Hannah More, a few slender volumes of bad verse by poets no one had ever heard of, and one severely mauled copy of *Pamela* taken from the circulating library in town. Its condition suggested that her ladyship either read with her teeth, or allowed Bubbums to have his way with the books. Many of the novels in our circulating library are similarly gnawed. The return date was marked as August 31, 1801. A mere decade and a half overdue. That was my pretext for calling, to return this long overdue library book, included in error with the others, which, presumably, did belong to the Weylins.

Prepared to be shunted into the small parlour, I had decided to shove the cursed necklace down the side of the settee, return *Pamela* when and if I was granted an audience – and I truly hoped I would not be – and leave at once. Seeton recognized me on the second visit.

'Is her ladyship expecting you?' he asked with his usual hauteur, but he let me in.

'No, she is not. Shall I wait in the other room?'

'One moment, please,' he said, and disappeared, not into the Blue Saloon, but down the hallway, leaving me to cool my heels just inside the door.

I made use of the time to examine the entrance for possible hiding places. Unfortunately, the decorations in that area were all statues, and I could not like to hang a string of diamonds around the neck of Zeus. While I was looking about for other hidey-holes, there was a light sound of footsteps, and Lord Weylin came wafting down the staircase. He was turned out in what he, no doubt, considered country style. He wore buckskins and top boots whose pristine condition suggested no familiarity with the great outdoors.

He stopped dead in his tracks and stared. 'Miss Barron,' he said, with a formal bow.

'Good morning,' I replied, backing away from Zeus, and blushing at the memory of our last encounter. At least he could not think I would try to slip a six-foot statue into my pocket.

'You have come to see Mama, I collect?'

'Yes, to return one of the books you were kind enough to send to the Book Society,' I said, holding out *Pamela*.

He looked at it, then lifted his eyes to gaze at me. 'You have an aversion to Richardson? A trifle racy, perhaps, but then, you are no longer a deb.'

That chronic air of disdain suggested he was seeking out crow's-feet and faded skin, and finding them in abundance. 'I merely thought you might prefer to return it to the circulating library, whence it came – fifteen years ago.'

'Overdue, is it?' He reached for the book and opened the gnawed cover. 'An oversight. Very kind of you to return it. You must go to the library and select a different novel.'

'I did not come to beg, Lord Weylin!' Yet if I left now, my job would still be unaccomplished. The library seemed a good place to hide the necklace. 'Well, perhaps if you have some novels you are finished with . . .'

He wafted his hand to indicate the library was down the hall-way. I said, 'Thank you,' and began to move along. Weylin followed behind to curtail my depredations on his library.

'I must commend you for your endeavors, Miss Barron. It is a good idea for you ladies to keep your minds busy,' he said, in a hatefully condescending way.

'Yes indeed, for we do not all have a dog to keep us occupied,' I replied. His head jerked around to look at me. I ignored it and kept walking.

When we reached the library, Lord Weylin stopped at the door. 'You may help yourself to any of those,' he said, gesturing toward a heap of books on a table. 'I am discarding them to make room for new books. One must keep abreast of the intellectual life. Philosophy, poetry . . .' He bowed and left, with a chilly smile.

One quick peek at the discards was enough to tell the tale. Bubbums had been tasting them all – and some of them were fine .books, too, with leather and gilt bindings. I took a quick look about the room to choose my hiding spot. The library was just that – a library and nothing more. All the walls were lined with books. There were two tables with chairs in the middle of the room, but I could hardly just lay the necklace on the table. There was a French door leading to a small garden bordered with yews, with a few rosebushes. The best I could come up with was to hide the necklace behind the books, and hope that it would be discovered in the near future. Those books had the neat, unused look of decorations. The necklace might lie undetected for a hundred years, until someone needed a quotation, or Bubbums got hungry.

I peered out the doorway and saw, across the hall and down a few yards, another room that offered more choices. It was a small room, whose sole function, so far as I could tell, was to provide a showplace for more Chinese porcelain. It held glass-fronted cabinets filled with all sorts and colors of vases. Perfect! Whatever of books, Lord Weylin did take an active interest in his porcelains, and would find the necklace. I darted to the nearest cabinet and tried the door, only to find it locked. I tried another cabinet, and another, until I had toured the room. Every one was locked up as tight as a safe.

Right in the middle of the room there was a big, square table with a porcelain horse and some other statuary on it; none of the items with a cavity, however. If Lord Weylin ever sat in this room, he sat on one of four wooden chairs with ladder backs and no padding. How was it possible I could not find a hiding place for a small necklace in the whole room?

I did not hear any footsteps in the hallway, which makes me wonder if Lord Weylin and his mama did not creep up on me to catch me out, stealing the vases. The first I learned of their presence in the library across the hall was the sound of excited voices. They were speaking in low tones, but with enough emotion that the words were audible.

'Where can she be?' Lord Weylin demanded. 'I left her here not five minutes ago.'

'Let us hope she has given up and gone home,' his mama replied sharply. 'It is clear as the nose on your face she is running after you, Algie. She never darkened our door for a quarter of a century, and the minute you get home, she is here every time you turn around. The gall of her!'

'It is not me she's after! She's trying to help herself to something from my collection. I knew I should not have submitted to that interview in the *Observer*. My insurance agent complained of it. The Chinese Room! I wager she's there!'

This was followed at once by the sound of running feet, and before I could recover from shock, Weylin came hurtling into the room at full tilt. I don't know which of us was more shocked and outraged. For a full sixty seconds we stood, glaring at each other like a pair of pugilists.

'So I was right!' he crowed.

'Your Chinese vases are safe from me, Lord Weylin. I did not come to steal—'

'What are you doing in here?' he barked. 'I left you in the library.'

'I did not realize I was supposed to be a prisoner there. You forgot to lock the door.'

'I am afraid I must ask you to turn out your pockets.'

I gasped in disbelief. 'How could I steal anything? You have all the cabinets locked.'

'So you were trying!' he exclaimed triumphantly.

It was the last straw. If he suspected thievery, let him know the real thief, and not suspect me. I had done my best to conceal Uncle's black character, but I would not go to jail for him. Lady Weylin chose that moment to join us. She looked a question at her son.

'I was right,' he said over his shoulder.

'Miss Barron! I am shocked at you!' Lady Weylin said in her severest voice.

I already had the troublesome necklace in my hand. The only way to escape without involving the constable was to hand it over. I held out my hand and opened the fingers slowly. 'I did not come to relieve you of your knick-knacks, Lord Weylin, but to return this. I believe it belonged to your late aunt.'

He took the necklace and looked at it, frowning. 'Where did you get this?'

'I found it at Hernefield when I was clearing out the tower room to turn it into a studio.'

Lady Weylin reached out and took the necklace. 'But where did you get it? This is my sister's necklace.'

'I have no idea how it came to be there,' I said. 'Steptoe found it in the bottom of a drawer.'

'Steptoe!' Lady Weylin exclaimed. She and Weylin exchanged a very strange, knowing look. 'But I had already let him go before Margaret's necklace was stolen. He was with the Pakenhams at that time.'

'Who else could it be?' Lord Weylin said uncertainly. 'I fear we must set the constable on him this time, Mama.'

'No! It was not Steptoe,' I said, very reluctantly. If he had stolen it, he would not have shown it to me. He would not have hidden it in my uncle's room, and if he had, he would have removed it sooner. Turning the room into my studio had been

37

discussed for weeks. I was interested to hear, of course, that he was apparently recognized as a thief. I think the Weylins might have warned us when we hired him.'

'How did it get there then?' Lady Weylin demanded.

'I cannot say.'

'Oh, come now, Miss Barron,' Lord Weylin said, in a jeering way. 'If you did not suspect some chicanery, you would have returned it in the normal way, instead of this game of cat and mouse. Your mama . . .' he said, examining me with some sign of pity.

'Certainly not! What we think, Mama and I, is that my uncle, Barry McShane, must have got hold of it somehow. It was found hidden in his dresser. Steptoe found it, but he made no effort to conceal it. He gave it to me, and told me it had belonged to Lady Margaret, which is why I – I have been – trying to return it.'

To my considerable astonishment, Lord Weylin put his sleek head back and emitted a very natural-sounding burst of laughter. 'We were both wrong, Mama,' he said. Then he put one hand on my elbow, the other on his mother's, and led us both back to the Blue Saloon.

'It is no laughing matter, Algie,' Lady Weylin said.

'It has its comical elements, though Miss Barron was not amused,' Weylin replied, shooting a peculiar glance at me.

We sat, Lady Weylin on her sofa with Bubbums at her feet, Lord Weylin and myself on the hard chairs. Weylin unbent enough to pour us a glass of excellent sherry.

'But what a delightful mystery!' he said, shaking the diamonds in his palm as if they were no more than a handful of salted nuts. 'How do you think your uncle got them?'

'He obviously stole them,' Lady Weylin said.

'Let us temper our judgment, Mama,' her son cautioned. 'One

false accusation can be an accident – and forgiven, I hope. To repeat the offence looks like harassment.'

Lady Weylin twitched at her shawl. I said, 'They were stolen at Tunbridge Wells, were they not? My uncle never went to Tunbridge Wells. He went often to London.'

'Perhaps he bought them there from a fence,' Lord Weylin suggested, peering at me for my reaction.

'Why would he do that?' his mother asked. 'He was not married. He had no lady friend to give them to, so far as I recall. Are you quite sure he used to go to London, and not Tunbridge Wells, Miss Barron? Algie tells me any number of lightskirts are at Tunbridge these days, on the catch for a patron. Your uncle used to have the reputation of a ladies' man. It was mentioned when he came back from India. The spinsters were all in a flutter.'

'No, he went to London,' I repeated, 'to visit friends at the East India Company.'

'Well, it is very odd,' Lady Weylin said. 'And that is why you have been landing in on us with regularity, Miss Barron?'

'That is the only reason I have called twice.' She made me sound like a poor relation seeking rack and manger.

'I cannot imagine why you made such a to-do of it. You should have told me the truth. I have no use for slyness. You need not fear legal proceedings, now that your uncle is dead and buried, eh, Algie? Margaret left her estate to you. It is for you to decide.' Lord Weylin nodded his agreement. 'We shall keep the matter hush,' she continued. 'The Barrons are a quite respectable family, after all. No point embarrassing your mama.'

'That is very kind of you, ma'am,' I said, feeling as if the weight of the world had fallen from my shoulders. 'We should have just returned the necklace and explained, but we were ashamed for Mr McShane.'

'Only natural,' she said. In her relief that I was not legging after her son, she became almost civil. And in my relief at not being prosecuted, I forgave her for that condescending 'quite respectable.'

I finished up my sherry quickly and took my leave. Lord Weylin accompanied me to the door, chatting as we went.

'I am sorry we were so swift to condemn you, Miss Barron, but your actions were . . . strange, to say the least.'

'Your reaction appeared equally strange to me, milord. Let us forget the matter,' I said, heading for the door.

'Let bygones be bygones,' he said, with a goodwill but a lamentable lack of originality. He did not follow me toward the door. I had the feeling he wished to detain me, for he continued talking. 'I was in London when Aunt Margaret had her necklace stolen. I thought, at the time, that I ought to have gone to Tunbridge, but my work in the House made it impossible. I daresay there is no point going at this late date.'

'I shouldn't think so. It all happened quite five years ago. There would be no hope of finding the culprit now.'

A frown of concentration hardened the lines of his face, and his dark eyes gleamed with intelligence. 'It happened in May, as I recall.'

'Yes, I first heard of it at the spring assembly.'

'You would not remember whether your uncle was in London at the time?'

The implication of his questions was becoming clear, and troublesome. 'I am afraid not. I did not record his visits in my diary,' I snipped.

A smile peeped out. 'You would have more interesting things to write there, no doubt.' He looked at my reticule. 'You are leaving empty-handed, Miss Barron.'

'I did not come to beg or borrow – or steal!'

His lips twitched in amusement. 'That ill-considered accusation was unforgivable. I am indeed sorry. I had very little idea of your character. . . .'

'We have been neighbors for twenty-five years, milord. If I were a thief, you would have heard a rumor of it before now.'

'Possibly, but in all those twenty-five years, I had not heard you have a quick temper, and a somewhat reckless manner of solving life's little problems. That was a shatterbrained thing to do, you know. I was within Ames-ace of sending off for the constable.'

'It is indeed strange how little we neighbors know of each other. I, for instance, had no notion who was responsible for all the damaged books in the library. I see now why they are called dog-eared.'

He cocked his head to one side and just looked at me for a long moment. 'A *very* quick temper,' he said. 'How did you manage to institute a quarrel, when I was only reminding you that you forgot to help yourself to the books I offered you? And about those library books – Mama is too lazy to replace them, but she does invariably pay for the damage. Come, let us select your novels.'

'You are very kind, milord, but it is really not literature a century old we are reading. It is the more recent novels. I suggest you consign your old books to the grate. They make a dandy fire on a cold evening.'

'I know it well. We discard so many books here. It requires patience to pull the leaves out. But what you were really saying, in your own way, is that I was palming rubbish off on you – and you are right.'

I was just trying to think of some polite way of agreeing and saying good-bye when Lady Weylin's fluting voice came from the Blue Saloon.

'Algie! I say, Algie! Bubbums wants to go out.'

The bored look that seized his features amused me. I wondered whether his mama and her Bubbums were not half the reason Weylin spent so little time at his home.

He said, 'Duty calls. If you think of anything that might help explain the mystery of the necklace, I wish you will let me know, Miss Barron. And I shall—'

'Algie? Are you there?'

He ignored the summons. 'And I shall let you know if I learn anything.'

'My uncle did not go to Tunbridge—'

'*Algie!*' The whine had escalated to a roar.

Lord Weylin called, 'Seeton, will you put the demmed dog out! I am trying to talk to Miss Barron.' He turned a sheepish face back to me. 'Sorry about that.'

'That is quite all right. Will you say good-bye to your mother for me?'

'Certainly, and I shall bark a farewell to Bubbums as well. Do you not plan to say good-bye to me, Miss Barron?'

'*Algie!*'

There was no longer any ignoring the summons. I escaped, before this domestic contretemps escalated into an argument. The visit had not gone at all as I had imagined, but at least the necklace was back where it belonged, and I had some ammunition to hold the hateful Steptoe in line until we found a replacement.

With Borsini's lesson to look forward to that afternoon and my studio to prepare for future lessons, I could enjoy the lovely spring day. There was just one troublesome little detail to mar perfection. *Had* Uncle Barry gone to Tunbridge Wells that May day five years before, and had he stolen Lady Margaret's necklace? It was pretty clear that Lord Weylin thought so, and he did not seem ready to let the matter rest.

Chapter Five

'Oh, Zoie, I wish you had not told them,' Mama scolded, when I returned and related the tale of my visit to Parham.

'It was that or let them believe I had gone to steal Lord Weylin's vases. In any case, it is over, Mama, and now we may have the exquisite pleasure of turning Steptoe off.'

'You say they knew all along he was a thief? Fancy their not letting us know. He might have robbed us blind.'

'We have been paying him an exorbitant salary, but that is our own fault. He has not filched the silver so far as I know.'

'I wonder he ever condescended to come to a house with so little worth stealing,' Mama said. 'Not that I mean we are poor, but after Parham, or even the Pakenhams, he would have slim pickings. I daresay the rich families all know what he is, and are in league not to hire him.'

While we were discussing the matter, Brodagan came sailing into the saloon, black eyes scowling. 'The luncheon meat is charred to cinders, meladies,' she announced with gleeful misery. There is little dearer to Brodagan's Irish heart than a catastrophe. The singed corners of her apron testified to dire doings below-stairs.

'I was such a gossoon as to leave Mary in charge of the meat, and the worthless creature betrayed me,' she continued. No blame is ever to be left in Brodagan's dish. Whatever she destroys, and she has a heavy hand, it is always the fault of someone else. Whether meat burns or pudding turns lumpy or gowns fall apart in the laundry, she can always shift the blame on to another. But really she is so devoted and such a worker that we are never savage with her.

She continued her litany of woe. 'Didn't I find her in the darkest corner of the dining room snuggling with Steptoe last night. I promised her ma I'd look after her. Either he goes or I go, for I'll not have my girls tampered with by the likes of him.'

'Send Steptoe in, Brodagan,' I said.

'Send him in, is it, and he in the tower rifling through Mr McShane's poor bits o' rubbish, thinking to find tuppence in a dead man's pockets. That's a good many stairs for my poor limbs to climb.'

'He is in the tower room now?' I asked.

'That's where he spent the morning, and no more clearing away done than if he'd stayed at the door, where he'd ought to have been. I wasn't hired to be answering the door. It was that Mrs Chawton who called, about the books.' She drew out a note and fought her way through it as if it were a patch of nettles. 'She says Guy Man . . . somebody, or was it Scott? Anyhow, it's sold out, and Vicar's wife don't care for the heathen, Lord Byre, or is it Berry? No matter, she said the fellow who wrote about little Harold. Mrs Dobbigan and Mrs Steele have already read every word of Maria Edgewool, and none of the other ladies like your idea of *Proud and Prejudiced*, by an onymous lady. I never trust an ominous lady. If she's afraid to put her name to her scribbling, you may be sure the book is no better than it should be.'

'Thank you, Brodagan. I shall deal with Mrs Chawton. I am sorry you had the inconvenience of looking after the door.'

'Your apron, Brodagan! You have singed it,' Mama said.

Brodagan stared placidly at her charred apron. 'There's two night's work and two shillings of me pittance of money gone up in flames, for I'll not disgrace you by being seen in this ruin again, meladies. It'll make dandy rags,' she said, and sailed out. Of course, she would cut off the burned edge and have Mary rehem it, but one did not introduce reality into one of her Celtic tragedies.

'I shall go up and bring Steptoe down for you to dismiss him, Mama,' I said.

Her pretty face pinched in displeasure. 'Why don't you speak to him yourself, dear? You handle him better than I.'

Mama dislikes trouble nearly as much as Brodagan relishes it. I fall in the middle, and am the go-between for such jobs as this. I did not look forward to confronting Steptoe, but I did not dread it either. I found him in the tower room, as Brodagan had said. He was separating my uncle's belongings into two boxes, one for the better items, one for the worn garments.

He looked up boldly. 'I'll keep this lot for myself,' he said, pointing to the box of good clothes. 'My tailor can do something with these jackets.'

'My tailor' – as though he were a fine gent! It was the little goad I needed to lend sharpness to my words. 'I have just returned from Parham, Steptoe. I told her ladyship where the diamonds were found. No legal action will be taken.' He looked sulky, but not so chastened as he ought. 'I am afraid we cannot see our way clear to increasing your salary. Naturally you will not want to remain with us at your present wage. You may consider yourself free to look for another position. It will be best if you not use us as a reference. Let us say two weeks, to give us both time to make other arrangements.'

His snuff-brown eyes narrowed. 'I might be able to get along on my present wage for the meanwhile,' he said.

'You force me to remove the gloves, Steptoe. Your services are no longer required.'

His reply was not apologetic, but aggressive. 'I never took nothing from you! You can't say I did.'

'I did not accuse you of stealing the spoons.'

'If it's that little Chinese jug from Parham you're referring to, I never took it. It got broken, and if one like it turned up at the antique store, it's nothing to do with me.'

It was foolish of him to actually tell me why he had been released from Parham. Nothing was more likely to vex Lord Weylin than tampering with his porcelains. 'Two weeks, Steptoe,' I said, and turned to leave, happy to put the unpleasant incident behind me.

'I wouldn't do that if I was you, miss,' he said, with a nasty smile in his voice. I turned and looked a question at him. 'I've a mate at Tunbridge Wells,' he said.

'What of it?'

'I go there on my holidays and days off. Interesting, what you see at Tunbridge.'

'If you have something to say, Steptoe, say it.'

'I'm not one to go rashly hurling accusations, like some. But I know what I saw at Tunbridge, and I know who I saw – the weekend Lady Margaret's necklace was stolen.'

I felt my body stiffen at his words. 'Are you referring to my uncle?'

His lips drew into a cagey grin. 'Will you still be wanting me to leave, miss?'

'There will be no salary increase,' I said, and left on that ambiguous speech.

Naturally I darted straight down to the saloon to tell Mama what had happened.

Mama paled visibly. 'He'll tell the world Barry was there when the necklace was stolen! Do you think it is true, Zoie?'

'Barry had the necklace. Lord Weylin asked whether I was certain Uncle did not go to Tunbridge. We don't really know where he went. We have only his word for it.'

'My own brother, a common thief!'

What bothered me more was what Lord Weylin would say if Steptoe told him. It was intolerable to be in the clutches of a creature like Steptoe. I had been looking forward to Borsini's visit, but this new development robbed it of all pleasure. I discussed the matter with Mama over lunch, and we decided we must go over all Barry's papers to see if we could find any evidence of his having been at either London or Tunbridge Wells. He might have receipts from hotels, or his bankbook might turn up interesting sums. The deposits should be no more than his pension from John Company. If larger deposits appeared, we would know the worst. We also hoped to discover what he had done with his ill-gotten gains, for when he died, his total estate of thirty-nine pounds went to Mama.

I wrote to Borsini, putting off his visit, and spent the afternoon in the attic with Mama, rooting through boxes of old letters and receipts. There was nothing to indicate any untoward doings. The recent bankbooks held only a record of the quarterly pension deposits. Uncle took nearly the whole sum out as soon as it went in. He kept a running balance in the neighborhood of fifty pounds. Whatever he spent the rest on, he must have paid cash.

Taking into account the small sum Mama took from him for room and board, though, he seemed to have spent a great deal of money. He did not indulge himself in a fancy wardrobe. He had a couple of decent blue jackets, one good evening suit, and one old-fashioned black suit that he never wore. It was quite ancient. He did not set up a carriage, or even a hack. On the few occasions when he rode, he borrowed my mount. He was not the sort to spend his nights in the taverns, or eat meals out. Mama thought it was the rumors of his Indian misadventure with the account books that kept him to himself. He felt it keenly.

Mama had perched on the edge of a trunk. She called, 'Look at this, Zoie. This is curious.' I went to see what had caught her interest. It was a bankbook dating back to the time of Barry's arrival at Hernefield. 'He came home with five thousand pounds! It was withdrawn from the bank the week after he got here. What did he do with it?'

I stared at the crabbed entries, counting the zeroes to make sure it was five thousand, and not five hundred, or fifty thousand. Nothing seemed impossible, but it was indeed five thousand. We puzzled over it awhile, until a dreadful apprehension began to form.

'Was he paying someone off, being held to ransom?' Mama suggested.

'Steptoe!' I exclaimed.

'Steptoe was still with the Pakenhams then. He only came to us three years ago. We cannot blame Steptoe, much as I should like to.'

'What is the date?' I said, running my eye along the left-hand column. 'May the fifteenth, 1811. About the time Lady Margaret's necklace was stolen. Mama, Uncle Barry *bought* the necklace! And here we were in a great rush to give it back to the Weylins.'

She clapped her two hands on her cheeks. 'Oh dear, and they will never believe us. I can hardly believe it myself. Five thousand pounds thrown away on that ugly old thing.'

'And to think I humbled myself to them, apologizing and listening to Lady Weylin accuse me of chasing after her son.'

'Why did Lady Margaret say it was stolen?' Mama asked. 'The thing was not entailed. Her husband gave it to her as a wedding gift, so if she wanted to sell it, she could. Barry must have bought it in all innocence from whoever stole it.'

'Why would he do that? It is not as though he got it at a bargain price. The necklace would hardly be worth five thousand, and to buy it from some hedge bird on a street corner – it makes no sense. If he wanted a diamond necklace for some reason, he would have bought it from a reputable jeweller.'

After considerable discussion, we had gotten no further toward solving the mystery.

'Steptoe knows something about this,' I said, and rose to march downstairs and confront him.

He was still in the tower room, which struck me as highly suspicious. As there was nothing there worth stealing, however, I only told him his duties were belowstairs, before speaking of the more important matter. I chose my words carefully. It was not my intention to tell him anything, only pick his brains to discover what he knew.

I jumped in without preamble. 'I want to know the meaning of your cryptic reference to Tunbridge Wells, Steptoe,' I said.

He looked at me with the face of perfect innocence, but with that sly light beaming in his eyes. 'Tunbridge Wells, madam? A fine and healthy spot. I often go there to take the waters. I believe I mentioned it to you earlier.'

'You implied seeing my uncle there. What was he doing?'

'I did not say I had seen Mr McShane, madam. You must have misheard me.'

'Then you did not see him?'

'Oh, I did not say that either, miss.' The subtle shift from 'madam' to the demeaning 'miss' did not pass unnoticed. 'It might come back to me anon.'

There was obviously no point quizzing him further. He knew something, but he was holding on to it for future mischief.

'Why are you wasting your time up here? Go downstairs. That is what we are paying you for.'

'Certainly, miss.'

His bow was a perfect model of impertinence. I wanted to run after him and kick him, but uncertainty held me in check. The devil knew something that would redound to my uncle's discredit, or he would not be so brass-faced. I went back to the attic and reported my failure to Mama.

My mood could hardly have been worse when Steptoe came tripping up to the attic ten minutes later. His bold eyes took a close look at what we were doing before he spoke. 'Lord Weylin to see you, Miss Barron.'

'Lord Weylin!' Mama exclaimed. 'What can he want?'

'He did not say, madam,' Steptoe said. 'Shall I tell him you are indisposed, Miss Barron?'

It was what I wanted to say, but I would not give Steptoe the satisfaction. 'Certainly not. I shall be down presently. Pray show his lordship into the saloon while I wash my hands.'

'I have already done so, madam.'

I gathered up my uncle's papers to take to my room, safe from Steptoe. 'Come down with me, Mama,' I said. 'I cannot meet Weylin alone.'

'Why, Zoie,' she laughed, 'it is not a courting call. It is only business. At your age there can be no impropriety in meeting a gentleman alone.'

'Of course it is not a courting call!'

'Well then – I shall just poke about up here and see what else I can find. Leave those papers with me.'

I left her to it and went to my room to freshen up.

Chapter Six

That killing phrase, 'at your age' has begun finding its way to Mama's lips too often to suit me. It seems only yesterday the phrase that guided my actions was 'when you are a little older'. When had I become old enough to be my own chaperon? The awful answer is that the point had not arisen in recent memory, because no gentleman had tried to get me alone.

Naturally I knew Lord Weylin had only come to discuss the curst necklace, but that did not mean I must greet him with dusty hands and cobwebs in my hair. With the memory of his sartorial elegance still fresh in my mind, I was tempted to change out of the three-year-old sprigged muslin I had put on for rooting in the attic. By the time I had washed up and brushed away the cobwebs, ten minutes had passed. I could not like to leave him waiting any longer, and went belowstairs in the old sprigged muslin.

Our saloon, which is not honored with a formal name like the Blue Saloon at Parham, suddenly seemed cramped and shabby. Lord Weylin's boots shone more brightly than our mirrors; his jacket had more nap than our matting. I wished I had changed my gown, but as I had not, I went forward to greet him.

He rose and bowed. 'Miss Barron. You will be wondering what

brings me pelting to see you so soon after your visit.' If he took any interest in either my hair or my gown, he concealed it well. His glowing eyes displayed a keen interest in something, but that something was not Miss Barron, nor her lack of a chaperon either.

'I am sure you are welcome any time, milord, but I expect I know why you are here. It is about the necklace.'

'Of course.'

His thoughtless 'Of course' confirmed that no other reason for coming had so much as entered his well-barbered head.

'The strangest thing!'

My heart plunged. He had heard something to Barry's discredit! Steptoe had sent him a note, or— For a moment, Lord Weylin faded to a black cloud, which slowly dissipated to reveal my caller, staring at me in astonishment. I did not quite tumble over, but I was reeling.

He hastened forward to assist me into a chair. 'What an idiot I am! I've frightened you to death. Let me get you a glass of wine. You're white as paper.'

He bustled about, pouring the wine and handing it to me. I sipped and was glad for the warmth it brought to my shaken body. 'A weak spell. I cannot think what came over me,' I said. 'Pray help yourself to a glass of wine, milord.' I wished we had set out a better wine. There were still a few bottles of Papa's good wine in the cellar, but the sherry on the table was first cousin to vinegar. He did not take any, however. His interest was all on the necklace.

He drew it out of his pocket and placed it on the table in front of me. With the recent discovery of Uncle's financial doings in my head, I jumped to the conclusion that he had discovered in some manner that Barry had bought it, and he was giving it back to us. 'How did you find out my uncle bought it? You must have been looking through your Aunt Margaret's accounts, as I have been looking into my uncle's.'

His brows rose in gentle arcs. 'I beg your pardon? Are you saying your uncle *bought* the necklace?'

'I . . . well, perhaps.' Then I said more firmly, 'Yes.'

'Will you explain more fully? I do not quite understand.'

I explained about the five thousand pounds Uncle had come home with, and taken out of his account at around the time the necklace had disappeared.

'Good God!' he exclaimed. 'It looks as though my aunt is the thief, for this thing she sold him is glass.'

'You mean it is not real diamond?'

'Mama thought it did not sparkle as it should. I tried cutting a windowpane with it. The edge of the stone crumbled without making a dint in the windowpane. I rushed it straight into the jeweller in Aldershot. Stacey confirmed that the thing is glass. Worth five or ten pounds.'

I was stunned into temporary silence. When I looked at the necklace again, it seemed to have lost its lustre. It looked common, cheap. I said, 'So your aunt never had a diamond necklace at all?'

'She had one, all right. She took it to Stacey to be cleaned shortly before it was stolen. This is a copy. Mama did not know of its existence, nor did I, though it is not uncommon for ladies to have copies made of their jewels.'

'And the real diamonds – they are still missing?'

'Yes, along with a few other baubles. Just trifles really. A garnet brooch, and an opal ring. The more valuable MacIntosh jewelry was entailed on MacIntosh's son.'

'Your aunt did not report the other items stolen?'

'No, which is odd, for she certainly made a fine ruckus when the necklace was taken. I confess it is all a complete mystery to me. And now you say five thousand pounds of your uncle's money has vanished as well?' Lord Weylin displayed the keenest interest in all of this. I did not think he was really concerned, or worried about the jewelry, but just interested in a bizarre little mystery.

'Actually it vanished shortly after he came to us.'

'Remind me, when was that, exactly?'

'He withdrew the money the fifteenth of May, 1811.' I looked to see if the date suggested anything to him.

'About the time my aunt's necklace disappeared – which is why you thought he'd bought it, of course. And no great bargain either. The thing was not insured, but it had been evaluated for insurance purposes at four thousand pounds. My aunt did not renew the policy as she so seldom wore it, and felt it was safe at Parham. When one takes into account that Mr McShane would be called a thief if he ever produced the necklace, it begins to look as though his purchasing it is not the answer.'

'He would never have bought it under those terms. Your aunt would not have claimed it stolen if she had sold it.'

We sat frowning at the glass beads on the sofa table in silence. 'Perhaps I shall have a glass of that wine,' he said, and helped himself. He was too gentlemanly to grimace at its sharp taste, but I noticed he set it aside after one sip and was in no hurry to take it up again.

After a frowning pause, he continued, 'It almost seems the two incidents are related – certainly by time, if not by place. You were here, and privy to your uncle's doings, Miss Barron. Had he anything to do with Lady Margaret?'

'To the best of my knowledge, they never exchanged more than a nod. She did not call at Hernefield, and we do not call at Parham. Uncle lifted his hat if they chanced to meet in town or at some social do.'

'And Mr McShane never went to Tunbridge Wells?'

I hesitated a moment before answering. The situation had changed since the morning, when I had humiliated myself by giving back the necklace. It was now Lady Margaret whose actions were under a cloud. I decided to reveal Steptoe's hint.

'I am not aware of his ever going there. Our butler, however, has dropped a dark hint that he saw my uncle at Tunbridge. I cannot get anything concrete out of him. He is the slyest dog in the parish.'

Lord Weylin nodded and said, 'Steptoe,' in a grim voice. 'Whatever possessed you to hire the man?'

'We would not have done so had you seen fit to warn us he is a thief,' I shot back. 'Really, milord, I think you might have warned us.'

He looked surprised at my sharp tone. 'I did caution the Pakenhams, when they inquired after his character. They were in urgent need of an experienced footman, and Steptoe knows his business. They took him on probation, with a warning. He behaved himself for two years, then small items began disappearing, and they let him go. Did they not caution you, when you spoke to them?'

'We did not speak to them. As he had worked at Parham, we felt he must be reliable. We offered him the post of butler; he was happy to be promoted from footman, and accepted. As you are our neighbor, I think you might have warned us.'

'Mama was concerned, but she did not feel he could do much harm here.' A look of chagrin seized his face the minute the words were out. 'That is – not that I mean—'

I quenched down an angry reproof. 'Hernefield is not so littered with chinoiserie as Parham, to be sure,' I snipped.

Lord Weylin wisely let the matter drop, and spoke on quickly to cover his gaffe. 'How did you learn of his having taken my Tang vase? I never could prove it, and was reluctant to publicly shame the man without proof, though I am morally certain he was the culprit.'

'He blurted it out himself. He thought we already knew.'

'I take it, then, that you have given him his *congé*?'

I blushed to admit we had not. 'It is this matter of his knowing something about Tunbridge Wells,' I explained. 'I hope to discover what it is he knows.'

'What can he know? He obviously saw your uncle there, and is trying to make gain on it.'

'Yes, but . . .' Lord Weylin just looked patiently while I sorted out my muddled thoughts. 'It is the *way* he says it, as though my uncle were doing something he should not.'

'You are letting him play on your susceptibilities, Miss Barron. I must own that surprises me,' he said with a small smile. 'You were more forthcoming at Parham. Stop a moment, and consider the facts. Mr McShane did not have the stolen necklace; he had a worthless copy. Did he leave a large sum of money in his Will? Is that what concerns you?'

'Certainly not; he did not even leave enough to bury himself. Everyone else who goes to India comes home a nabob, but Uncle only brought back five thousand pounds, and he lost that, or gave or gambled it away.'

'Then it does not appear he was engaged in any criminal doings. Would you like me to have a word with Steptoe?'

'It will do no good. When I tried to quiz him, he as well as denied having said anything to me. The man is a weasel.'

'You should dismiss him at once.'

'I daresay you are right. Now that I know that necklace is glass, I shan't hesitate to do it.'

Weylin glanced at his watch, and said, 'I must be running along.' He picked up the necklace, looked a question at me, and when I did not object: he put it in his pocket.

I said, 'I still think it odd my uncle had the copy.'

'It is one of life's little mysteries.'

'He must have obtained it at Tunbridge Wells, don't you think? If he and Lady Margaret ever had anything to do with each other, it did not happen here.'

'I suggest we let sleeping dogs lie,' Weylin said, rising in a smooth motion. 'There is nothing to be learned at this late date. I have business in London tomorrow, so I shall take my leave of you, Miss Barron. I shall risk boring you by repeating what I said earlier. If you learn anything more of this business, I wish you will let me know, and I shall also tell you if I chance across anything.'

I murmured a vague agreement, and he left. I sat on, mulling over the matter. To Lord Weylin, with London and his politics to distract him, the affair of the necklace was a mere curiosity. For me, it loomed larger than that. I felt my uncle, and ultimately Mama, had been bilked of that missing five thousand pounds. The secret was buried at Tunbridge Wells. A trip there was well worth the effort. And to ensure smooth sailing, Weylin would be in London, well removed in case I learned something to Barry's discredit.

It was equally possible that Lady Margaret was no better than she should be, in which case I would not hesitate to inform him. The idea had not quite been put to rest that the illustrious Lady Margaret had conned my uncle into buying a fake necklace, and sold the genuine article in or around Tunbridge Wells. Would Barry have been fool enough to fall in with a bargain like that? Had Lady Margaret been younger and prettier, she might have hoodwinked him, but she was a stout matron – stylish to be sure, but with little left of her beauty. I was sorry I had let Weylin walk off with the glass beads in his pocket. They might jar someone's memory at Tunbridge Wells.

I jumped up to go after him, and noticed that he was still in the hallway, talking to Steptoe. They had their heads together like conspirators.

'Is there something amiss, Lord Weylin?' I asked, stepping toward them.

'I shall see myself out, Steptoe,' he said to the butler. Steptoe darted off.

'I was just quizzing him a little,' Lord Weylin explained. 'As I suspected, he saw nothing at Tunbridge Wells. He knew my aunt used to go there, and was trying to frighten you. I fear there is nothing to be learned at Tunbridge.' He gave the sort of measured look a cat gives, just before leaping on a mouse.

'Indeed, there is no point in going all the way to Tunbridge,' I agreed. He was the last person I wanted to go there.

We exchanged good days, and he left. After he was gone, I remembered I had not gotten the necklace back from him.

Chapter Seven

Mama and I set out for Tunbridge Wells at nine the next morning, despite an early shower that promised to destroy our trip. She was not hard to convince once I had related the gist of Lord Weylin's visit, and held out the lure of recovering her brother's five thousand pounds. She was firmly convinced that Lady Margaret had taken advantage of Barry's susceptibilities.

'He was always putty in the hands of a lady,' she said, as the carriage rumbled through the mist.

'I never saw any evidence of weakness for ladies, Mama. He scarcely looked at them.'

'He used to, when he was younger. A leopard does not change his spots. She fed him some tale of woe that she needed the money, and he, like a regular green-head, handed over every penny he had in the world. And to think—'

To divert the story of her paying for his coffin, I said, 'Lord Weylin says no such sum appeared in Lady Margaret's bank statements. Surely Uncle Barry was not such a gudgeon.'

We were back to the unanswerable question. 'Where did the money go, then?' she demanded.

These thoughts had been running around in my head for hours, and when the rain let up, I put them aside and enjoyed the scenery. The carriage progressed through pretty countryside, all gleaming from the recent downpour that left the leaves dripping with crystal pendants of rain. The sun came out, striking each droplet and broadcasting tiny prisms. Borsini would have enjoyed it. He could turn his brush with equal effect to either landscape or the human form. I regretted missing my lesson.

With a longish luncheon stop to rest Mama's aching bones, our trip took seven hours. It was four in the afternoon when we entered that picturesque, hilly moorland where Surrey turns into Kent, with Tunbridge Wells nestled in its folds. We hired a room at Bishop's Down Hotel, behind the Pantiles and facing the Common. It was late in the day to begin making inquiries, but we strolled out to see something of the town before darkness descended. At Tunbridge, one goes to the promenade called the Pantiles, where all society struts to see and be seen.

The height of the season is from July to September, but already in early June there was no shortage of tourists. The serious-minded folks who came for their health were not of much interest to me, even 'at my age'. An air of propriety hangs over the town, encouraged by such biblical names as the Mount Ephraim Hotel, and even Zion. Despite all this, there was a smattering of light-skirts, come to prey on the elderly gents.

We went to the Pantiles and duly admired the beauty of a colonnade on one side, a row of lime trees on the other. I had some hope of getting into the shops, but Mama felt the need of the chalybeate waters for her aching joints, so we went to the Pump Room, and paid one farthing each for a glass of impotable mineral water, which left us longing for a nice cup of tea.

As soon as Mama finished her water, we left to walk the length of the promenade before returning to our hotel to rest and change for dinner. It was just in front of King Charles the Martyr Church that we met Lord Weylin. Had we seen him first, I would have darted into a shop, and he would have done the same had his eyes been sharper. But we spotted each other at the same instant. Our eyes met, we both stared, caught between shame and anger. He swallowed his annoyance and came pacing forward, forcing a rictuslike smile onto his face.

I had barely time to warn Mama before he was making his bows. While I despised his duplicity, I could not but admire the smooth manner in which he carried off the embarrassing meeting. There is something to be said for breeding after all.

Without a blink of embarrassment, he said, 'Ladies, what a delightful surprise. I am just on my way to London, and stopped off on the chance of discovering some clue to our mystery.'

London, I need hardly say, is north-east of Aldershot. Tunbridge Wells is south-east. One does not require much geometry to know that the shortest distance between two points is a straight line, and not a trip around a right angle.

'We have just been trying the water,' I replied blandly.

'You are brave.' He smiled.

'We are on our way to our hotel,' was my next effort at civility.

'I shall walk along with you. Where are you staying?'

'Bishop's Down.'

His smile grew more strained by the moment. 'I am putting up there myself,' he said.

'Oh, then you are not proceeding to London today!' I exclaimed, in no joyful way. 'I understood you had urgent business there.'

'Politics is seldom urgent. Like the mills of the gods, Whitehall grinds slowly.'

'But it grinds exceedingly small,' Mama said. She is a keen devotee of Longfellow.

Weylin laughed as though it were a famous joke and replied, 'I don't know about that.' That eruption of laughter told me he was quite as embarrassed as I at being caught out in his lie.

He did not offer his arm, but he walked between us toward the hotel and at the corner put his hand on Mama's elbow, which she later said was very prettily done. She had not thought him so obliging.

As we walked along, not a word was mentioned about what had really brought us all to this resort of valetudinarians. Lord Weylin inquired how the Book Society was coming along, and I confessed that no major strides had been made during the twenty-odd hours since our last meeting. He mentioned Mrs Radcliffe as an author who might appeal to the ladies. I said that we had all enjoyed her gothic tales very much in our youth, but were interested in more worthwhile literature now.

He peered down and said, 'In your youth! I don't see any grey hairs, Miss Barron.'

Mama informed him I was a quarter of a century old. He examined my face as minutely as our brisk pace allowed. When we came to the next corner, I felt his hand at my elbow, but as it fell away as soon as we reached the safety of the walkway, I was forced to conclude it was my advanced state of decrepitude that occasioned the gesture.

We were soon at the hotel. We thanked Lord Weylin for his escort, and were about to escape when he gave a frustrated *tsk* and said, 'This is foolishness. Why are we treading on eggs? We all know why we are here. Let us get our heads together and see what can be done about finding the necklace.'

'We are not looking for your aunt's necklace,' I said. 'We are trying to discover what happened to my uncle's money.'

'Five thousand pounds,' Mama said importantly.

'Presumably the two are mixed up somehow. Money, however, is anonymous. Once in circulation, it is indistinguishable from any other money. A unique necklace, on the other hand, might be traced, and might have some bearing on Mr McShane's money. What do you say, ladies? Shall we discuss it over dinner? I have hired a private parlour, and would be delighted if you would be my guests.'

'I daresay there is no harm in it,' Mama said, with an uncertain glance at me. Lord Weylin seemed quite surprised at this luke-warm acceptance.

I said, 'We would be very happy to join you, milord.'

'I shall be waiting for you here in the lobby at seven.'

We thanked him and hastened along to our rooms. When we were behind closed doors, Mama said, 'I do not look forward to dining with Weylin. It is a pity we agreed. I don't suppose I could claim a sick headache, and we could eat in our room?'

'We shan't do much good locked in our rooms, Mama. Weylin is right. The necklace will be easier to trace than the money, and it might lead us to some clue.'

Mama cast a knowing look at me. 'You are setting your cap at him, in other words. I take leave to tell you, Zoie, he has no inter-est in a lady your age.'

'I am not setting my cap at him! And furthermore, he is a good decade older than I.'

'He is only thirty-one.' (*Only* thirty-one, you see. A gentleman close to a third of a century is a mere bantam cock, while a lady was an old hen at twenty-five.) 'Your papa remembered very well the day he was born. Old Lord Weylin set off fireworks at Parham. His mama had been trying for half a dozen years to produce a pledge of her love, and was afraid it would be a girl when she finally managed to become enceinte. Everyone came from miles around to see the baby. It was the talk of the parish.'

'Was there a large star in the sky to guide them to Parham that night?' I asked.

Mama sniffed her displeasure at such a sacrilegious joke. Still, if I had had any notion of setting my cap at Lord Weylin, that story would have stopped me. A man whose birth was announced with a public display of fireworks was obviously above my touch. Not that I had planned to chase after him, but when an eligible man crosses the path of a lady *my* age, it is only natural to consider it.

We had an hour's rest before changing for dinner. I spent the time planning how we might set about discovering any clues to the vanished necklace and money. Really it was a good thing Weylin had joined forces with us, because he might at least know where his aunt stayed in Tunbridge Wells. As he was staying at Bishop's Down, it seemed that his aunt might have stayed here, too. We could question the staff as to whom she met. A tour of the jewelry shops and pawnshops was another possible lead, in case she had hawked the necklace. No doubt Weylin had brought the copy with him, which might serve to jog the jewelers' memory. That was why he had taken it!

What I could not think of was any manner of finding out what had become of Barry's money. It would be just like life if Lord Weylin, who had no need of more wealth, should recover his prize while Mama and I went home empty-handed.

Mama fell into a light nap. At six-thirty I shook her awake and we both made our toilettes for dinner. Not knowing how long we would remain, I had brought two evening gowns with me. I wore the better of them for dinner with Lord Weylin. Borsini had talked me into wearing gowns of a classical design, to go with my 'classical' face. Mama calls my draped toga-like white crape with gold ribbons around the hem a shroud, and tells me I look a quiz. In fact, I have received several compliments on it, and thought a sophisticated gentleman like Lord Weylin might not despise it.

'Oh, Zoie, you are not wearing the shroud!' Mama exclaimed, when she looked up from her own toilette to see what I had on.

'We are only going down to Weylin's private parlour, Mama. No one will notice what I wear.'

'He will notice.'

'But then, we have agreed I am not chasing after him.'

'And a good thing it is, for you look a quiz, Zoie. Ever since you began those painting lessons, you have let your wardrobe fall into a shambles. And your hair looks very odd, too, in that funny old knot. I have not seen one like it since we buried Grandmama. I hope we do find Barry's money, for you will need every penny of it to nab a husband.'

'It is too late to change now,' I said crossly, and went downstairs with my confidence in tatters. It requires confidence to carry off a new and different style. I feared I looked ridiculous, and wished I had not worn the shroud, but was too stubborn or proud to change.

A very elegant-looking female stopped and turned around to examine me as we crossed the lobby. Her expression was not one of mirth, but of interest. The little incident brought my confidence back. When Lord Weylin came toward us, I met him with my head high, and a civil smile on my face.

Chapter Eight

I was aware of Lord Weylin's eyes examining me in a way they had not bothered to do before. His face wore an impassive, polite smile, but the eyes betrayed at least a latent interest in me as a woman. They lingered a moment on my black hair, before moving slowly to my eyes, and lips. I think it was the 'shroud' that first caught his attention. Borsini describes it as 'clinging to the womanly outlines of the body'. But Weylin was too polite to let his gaze rest on my anatomy.

'Ladies, may I compliment you both on looking particularly lovely this evening,' he said, with a bow.

He took my arm as well as Mama's to lead us to his private parlour. 'I have ordered wine and looked over the menu,' he said, 'but have waited for you before ordering. The burgundy – or perhaps champagne. Champagne goes with any viands.' His warm gaze suggested the champagne was a complement to my gown.

Mama said, 'You are extravagant, milord! Champagne!' as if we had never tasted this rarity. We had an excellent wine cellar when Papa was alive.

Not wishing to ally myself with her provincial sentiment, I examined the menu and chose the sole, with chicken to follow.

Mama said, 'That sounds good,' and had the same thing. Lord Weylin urged lobsters and crab and I don't know what all on us, but eventually settled for the sole and roast beef himself.

When the wine was poured, he raised his glass and said, 'To our success. May we all leave here richer.'

Even in that I spied out a compliment. It was the way he said it, with a secret smile at me. That smile suggested there were other sorts of riches than gold and diamonds.

'To our success,' I repeated, and we all drank.

The auspicious beginning made no progress after the first glass of champagne. Once we had our fish before us, we reverted to discussing business.

I said, 'I was wondering, Lord Weylin, as you have come to Bishop's Down, if this is the hotel where your aunt stayed when she was in Tunbridge.'

'Just so. This is where she told Mama she stayed. I made inquiries as soon as I arrived, and was told she had been here several years ago, but she has not been here for five years – about the time the necklace disappeared. Yet she continued coming to Tunbridge often, much oftener than before. She only came once a year for the first five years she was with us. Later on, she came four times a year, at the beginning of January, April, July, and October. She was getting older, of course, and might have had more need of the chalybeate waters. Still, that regular timing is interesting.'

Mama dropped her fork and exclaimed in a loud voice, 'It certainly is! Barry used to go to London four times a year, once a season, at about those same dates.'

Weylin stared at her with his jaw hanging slack. 'Is that a fact? By God, I think we are on to something here.'

'It is certainly a coincidence,' Mama agreed, 'but I doubt it can be more than that, for they scarcely knew each other. There would be no reason to hide it if they were friends. They were both single, and free to do what they wanted, even marry.'

'Barry took the five thousand from his bank on May the fifteenth,' I said. 'That date does not coincide with the date of his visits.'

'But he must have spent the money here,' Mama said. 'He certainly did not spend it at Hernefield.'

'Does something special occur on those dates?' I asked. 'I am thinking of some item of interest that could have taken them both from home. Horse-races, or meetings of some kind.'

'There would be no races in the dead of winter,' Weylin said. 'We must discover what other treats the area offers. Margaret was fond of the theatre, for instance.'

'Surely she would go to London for that,' Mama said. 'London is not much farther from Parham than Tunbridge Wells is. Barry's only interest in the theatre was the green room.'

Over our chicken and roast beef I mentioned my idea of visiting the various jewelry stores and pawnshops. Weylin said he had planned to do that. 'You must have wondered why I wanted the glass copy of the necklace,' he said.

'Yes; in fact, I went into the hall to ask you for it before you left Hernefield, but when I saw you with Steptoe, I forgot about it.'

'Steptoe,' he said. 'He knows something, I think.'

'Did he say anything to you?' I asked at once.

'Nothing of any account, but he wore the same oily look he wore when he told me he hadn't seen my Tang vase. The dealer he sold it to would not identify him. I suspect they were in collusion.'

'If Steptoe knows anything, what can he hope to gain by not telling us?' Mama asked.

'He is waiting for us to bribe him,' I said.

Weylin shook his head. 'I've already tried that. If we have no success here, our next move will be to have Steptoe watched, have him followed when he leaves Hernefield.'

Mama said, 'You might insert an advertisement in the *Tunbridge Journal*, asking any friends of Lady Margaret to be in touch with you. She must have had friends here, since she came so often, and over such a long period of time.'

'Now, that is an excellent idea!' Lord Weylin exclaimed. Mama blushed and simpered like a Bath miss.

'And her companion, milord – surely she did not come here unaccompanied.'

'Her companion was a Mrs Riddle, an old family retainer. She returned north when my aunt died. I did write to her before leaving Parham, but I do not expect a reply for some time. I did not have her address, and wrote in care of Angus MacIntosh. That is my aunt's stepson, who inherited his father's estate. Can you make inquiries of Mr McShane's valet, or groom, or—'

Mama shook her head. 'Barry used to travel alone, on the stage. He did not have a valet. When he needed a carriage, he used mine, but he did not take it when he left town, of course, for we needed it ourselves.'

'Pity. Had he any close friends. . . ?'

'Not in England,' Mama said. 'We are from Ireland, and he went from there to India. He stuck pretty close to home when he came to live at Hernefield, except for his trips to London.'

'Or possibly Tunbridge Wells,' I said. 'We shall make inquiries at the desk to see if Uncle stayed here.'

Lord Weylin said, 'If he did, he used some other name. I looked over the registers for the past five years. His name is not there, but there are plenty of hotels in the city. We shall ask around while we are here. A pity we hadn't a picture of him. I brought an ivory miniature of Aunt Margaret.'

He drew it from his pocket and showed it to us. I had not realized Lady Margaret had been a beauty in her youth. I gazed at a blue-eyed blonde lady with soft eyes and a charming smile.

'I doubt anyone would recognize her from this,' I said, handing it on to Mama.

'Not at a glance, certainly,' Lord Weylin agreed, 'but an old friend would recognize her.'

'Oh yes, I recognize her,' Mama said. 'She was certainly a beauty. Unfortunately, I do not have any picture of Barry at all.' Then she gave her cheek a light slap and laughed. 'Our wits are gone begging, Zoie. You must have taken Barry's likeness a dozen times. Did you keep any of those sketches?'

'I have half a dozen of them in one of my old sketchpads. I wish I had thought to bring one with me.'

'You can send to Hernefield and ask the servants to send you one,' Lord Weylin suggested.

'That would take a few days,' Mama said, pursing her lips. 'We had not planned to stay so long, milord. And you are in a hurry to get on to London, too.'

Lord Weylin was in no hurry to leave. 'I cannot like to leave this mystery unsolved,' he said. 'It is not just finding the necklace, though that is worth a few days. It is the uncertainty, the niggling feeling that Aunt Maggie was up to something naughty, that intrigues me. Can you not remain a few days? It might mean the recovery of your brother's money, Mrs Barron.'

'Aye, or it might mean finding out he was no better than he should be,' she said uncertainly.

Lord Weylin took it for a great joke, and after a few flattering remarks that she had been extremely helpful, he sweet-talked Mama into sending to Hernefield for my sketch and remaining to continue looking into the mystery.

Between the three of us, we demolished two bottles of champagne and enough food to make us uncomfortable. When dinner was finally over, Mama said, 'I feel like a Strasbourg goose. If I can make it up those stairs, I shall go straight to bed.'

'As soon as you have written to Hernefield for the sketch of your brother,' Lord Weylin said, shaking a playful finger at her. 'In fact, why waste time with letters? I can hire a mount and have one of my footmen ride there tonight. He can be back before morning.'

'He would have to ride all night!' Mama exclaimed.

'It is only fifty miles. On a good mount, he'll be there in two or three hours. Why do you not write the note now, ma'am, while I arrange for the mount, and give my footman his instructions?'

Mama looked lost at such a hasty way of carrying on. I confess I was favorably impressed. Weylin had always seemed an idle sort of gentleman, taking life pretty easily, but when he set his mind on something, he threw his whole energy into it.

'I had best write the letter,' I said. 'I know which sketchpad is required, and where it is. Brodagan will not like to be disturbed at such a late hour. I shall hint that the sketch might inconvenience Steptoe. That will ensure her compliance.'

Mama agreed to this and we parted, Weylin to speak to his footman, I to write the note, and Mama to sit waiting impatiently for Weylin's call, so that she might undress and go to bed. Shortly after nine he came tapping at the door.

'There is a band playing on the Pantiles,' he said, pocketing my note. 'Would you ladies like to take a stroll and hear it? It is a bit early to turn in.'

'Very kind, Lord Weylin,' Mama said, 'but I could not make it down those stairs again. I am a martyr to the rheumatism.'

'I am very sorry to hear it, ma'am.' Then his grey eyes turned to me, with a question. 'Miss Barron? Are your joints up to tackling the stairs?'

'I should enjoy a little exercise after that large dinner,' I said, looking to see if Mama objected to being left alone in a strange hotel.

I think she was glad to be rid of me. 'Try not to make a racket when you come in, Zoie. I shall be sleeping.'

'I shan't be late,' I promised.

'Not *very* late,' Lord Weylin said in an undertone. There was laughter in his eyes as he settled my shawl around my shoulders and offered his arm to lead me out.

The idea flashed into my mind that Lady Margaret was not the only one of his family who could be naughty when she felt like it. And Uncle Barry might not be unique in that respect in my own family either. There is some charm in being away from home, some slight relaxing of the social constraints. Perhaps it is no more than the knowledge that friends and neighbors are not watching, and so one can cut loose a little. Was that why Barry and Aunt Margaret came here?

Chapter Nine

Lord Weylin's footman, rigged out in dark green livery with gold trim, was waiting in the lobby. His eyes opened wide as a barn door to see me there with his master. It would not be long until the whole neighborhood at home heard about it. Weylin gave him the note for Brodagan, and he left.

'You realize that being seen here alone with me puts your reputation in jeopardy,' Weylin said, in a joshing way.

I replied in the same manner, 'So I assumed when your servant's chin hit the floor. This is too dainty a morsel for him to keep to himself.'

'I shall expect you to do the right thing by me if I am cast out of polite society,' he said, and we began walking toward the door.

'Are you referring to a character reference, sir? A sworn affidavit of your unexceptional behavior – or an offer of marriage?'

After the heedless words were out, I feared Weylin might think I was making a premature leap at the altar, but he laughed lightly and changed the subject.

'Lovers would have to be naïve indeed to think they could get away with clandestine meetings in a public hotel. A love nest is more usual.' He inclined his head toward mine and added, still in that laughing way, 'Or so I am told. Naturally a well-behaved gent like myself has no firsthand knowledge of such carrying on.'

'Of course not. And fish are but inferior swimmers, too, having heard of it only at second hand.'

The doorman held the door for us, and we went out into the warm evening, along the path to the Pantiles. It was a particularly clear night. The moon shone as brightly as a lantern, and a myriad of stars twinkled all across the heavens.

'June is a lovely month, is it not?' Lord Weylin said, in a pensive way. 'Summer looms before you, always promising more than it delivers.'

'April is my favorite month. I prefer the coming of spring, after a long, cold winter. If it promises more than it delivers, at least it does deliver summer.'

'Spring is too uncertain. One never knows whether he will awaken to frost or rain or sunshine. Rather like a visit with Miss Barron,' he added mischievously.

This was the nature of our conversation as we continued along to the Pantiles. There was a definite whiff of romance in the air. It seemed strange to see the colonnade lit up as brightly as daytime, with some of the shops still open for business, and the streets full of strollers. We continued along to where a band was playing. A crowd of holidayers had gathered around. Ladies – and I do not mean the word satirically – were flirting quite openly with gentlemen.

I noticed Lord Weylin was looking at them and said, 'There is something about being in a strange town that encourages loose behavior.'

One brow lifted and he replied, 'I have not observed our little trip having that effect on you, Miss Barron.'

'I daresay if those young ladies were accompanied by their mamas, they would not be working their fans so assiduously.'

'Your mama is not with you now,' he said, while his fingers tightened possessively on my arm.

If his lordship had some notion of instituting a flirtation while away from home, he was out in his reading of my character. I did not want a clandestine romance, carried on behind society's back. 'Shall we continue our walk?' I said coolly. 'The reason we came out was to get a little exercise. We are not making much headway standing here.'

'I noticed the lack of headway,' he murmured, and we continued on toward the church. 'How does it come you and I are not better acquainted, Miss Barron, having been neighbors for years?'

'I blame it on the infrequency of elections,' I replied. 'The only time you are at Parham is when an election is called.'

'But as we are neighbors, surely it does not require a national election to get you to call?'

'You forget, milord, I called on you twice this very week. There is just a little something in a threat to call the constable that makes one think twice before calling again. The road travels both ways. You have never called on me.'

'I have apologized about the vase. Can we not forget it?'

'You are the one who asked why I do not call at Parham.'

The air of flirtation was noticeably lacking in the remainder of our walk. After a longish pause, Weylin said, in the hearty way of a bored gentleman making conversation, 'So you are interested in sketching, Miss Barron.'

'Yes, I always enjoyed it, since I was a child. A few years ago I began taking lessons from Borsini. He is an Italian conte,' I added, and wished I had not, for it sounded like vulgar boasting.

Weylin's lips moved unsteadily. 'I have heard of him.'

'Perhaps you are familiar with his painting of the Prince Regent?'

'Very familiar. He tried selling one to me. He paints Prinney with monotonous regularity, and it is a pity the prince has never accepted any of the likenesses.'

'Are you saying Borsini was not commissioned? He just painted the picture for his own amusement?'

'No, for money. He runs a profitable sideline hawking copies of Sir Thomas Lawrence's profile of Prinney, but of course, that was not the one he tried to sell to the prince. I do not mean to disparage the man. One has to make a living, after all, and the copies are good enough in their way. There is such a surfeit of art teachers at the moment that he has trouble getting students.'

I felt quite deflated, and very vexed with Count Borsini. He had certainly given me the idea he was commissioned to do that painting of the prince. He had also claimed it was a great favor that he condescended to take me on as a student. It was only my unique talent, he said, that convinced him to do it. I had always found it odd that he moved to Aldershot, if he was in such high demand in London.

I twitched my shawl angrily about my shoulders and said, 'Shall we go back now? It is becoming rather chilly.'

'I thought we might stop for a glass of wine at those tables they have set up around the bandstand.'

'Two bottles of champagne were sufficient for me, thank you.' I set a brisk pace back toward the other end of the Pantiles.

'Is there some particular reason why we are running?' Weylin asked.

'It is chilly,' I repeated.

He made no reply, but he took his handkerchief from his pocket and wiped his brow, to show me his idea of the chilly weather. We went directly back to the hotel. I kept thinking all the way of how Borsini had duped me. Even now I was having the tower room made into a studio. Vanity, all vanity. Borsini had half

76

convinced me I was a genius, and I had gone along with it, paying him a fortune for his lessons.

As we entered, Lord Weylin said, 'I am sorry if I have offended you in some manner, Miss Barron. If some of my remarks were slightly out of line, can you not blame it on our being tourists, and forgive me?'

'I am not offended by you, Lord Weylin.'

'Then I should dislike to see you when you were offended! If you are not, then join me for a nightcap. I have a favor I want to ask of you. I have reserved the parlour for my use while I am here. We need not have wine. I am not trying to get you inebriated, after all. A posset, or cocoa . . . There can be no mischief in that.'

Since I was curious to hear what favor he wanted, I agreed. My ire was not directed at him, but at Borsini. He ordered tea, and while waiting for it, I asked what he wanted of me.

He placed the miniature of his aunt on the table and said, 'Would it be possible for you to do a sketch of my aunt as she looked before she died? Perhaps with this to assist your memory, you might fill out the cheeks, add a few chins, change the hair-style, and so on. Then we would have a recognizable likeness of her to show around – ask at the various hotels if anyone had seen her. If she used an alias, just checking the registers will be of no help.'

I examined the little ivory. 'The jowls had sagged, and the eyelids had drooped somewhat when I knew her,' I said, really talking to myself. 'The nose tends to become more prominent with age. Yes, I think I could do it quite easily.' Comparing my mental picture of Lady Margaret with the pretty girl in the minia-ture, I said, 'It is sad, is it not, to think how short a time beauty lasts?'

'It has long been one of the poets' main themes.'

Our tea arrived. I poured. 'Just a little milk, no sugar,' Weylin said. I had not planned to fix his tea for him; it seemed intimate somehow, but it seemed foolish to object, so I did it.

'Herrick wrote in that vein,' I said. ' "Gather ye rosebuds while ye may" – is that what his poem was called?'

'The title was "To the Virgins to Make Much of Time", I believe. Shakespeare covered the same ground in his sonnets. It is a poetic thought.'

'Yes, and it is a pity the poets usually debase it by making it a pretext for urging dalliance on the ladies.'

Weylin did not come to the rescue of his sex, but just smiled at the little picture of his aunt. 'I suppose we can rule out any romantic doings between your uncle and my aunt? They were several years past it, I should think.'

'Barry had a reputation for being a dasher in his youth, but I fear the fires were well banked by the time he returned to England. Mrs Delancey tried to entice him, but he paid her no heed, and she was attractive, too. Do you think Lady Margaret . . .'

He shook his head. 'I shouldn't think so. She was not a romantical sort of lady. She made a marriage of convenience – and that was in her youth, when the blood should have been at the boil if it was ever going to be.'

'If it were not for my uncle having the copy of the necklace, I would think it impossible the two had a single thing to do with each other. They did not move in the same circles.'

'The copy, and Steptoe's leering looks,' Weylin agreed. 'It seems to me this mystery is about money, not romance. Had they met twenty-five or thirty years ago . . .'

'But your aunt was in England, and my uncle was in Ireland.'

Weylin sat, frowning at the little ivory. 'Did your mama not say she recognized this likeness of Margaret, when I showed it to her? I am sure she did. Yet she came to England after my aunt had left. She could not have seen Margaret at this age.'

'She must have meant she recognized the features of the older lady in this likeness,' I said, puzzling over what Mama had said. 'That must be it, but I shall ask her.'

'Please do. I don't know why it is, but this little mystery intrigues me. Perhaps it is just a welcome relief from the tedium of politics.'

'I expect you should be returning to Whitehall soon.'

'I will be a better politician for this brush with reality. We sometimes lose track of human emotions, with all our fine rhetoric about the lot of the common man.' He looked at me and smiled. 'Perhaps I should invite the neighbors to Parham more often than each election year.'

'That would be a beginning. The local lord ought to have balls. We do not have enough balls.' As this was perilously close to admitting how limited my romantic doings were, I added, 'You seem more . . . human already.'

'You seem more human now, too, Miss Barron. I shall take my courage in my hands and ask why you were so out-of-reason cross with me during our walk. I thought we were making some headway, then suddenly you pokered up as though I had done something ill bred – like accusing you of stealing,' he said, with a teasing look.

I could not like to admit how Borsini had gulled me, and made a bantering reply. 'Why, you are very sensitive, milord. I am sure I did not say anything to offiend you.'

'Silence can be offensive, too. You were running too fast to speak. You could not wait to get away from me. Shall I tell you what I thought of the matter?' he asked slyly.

'Please do.'

'I thought you had suddenly remembered something to your uncle's discredit, and wanted to conceal it from me.'

'It had nothing to do with that! I told you, I was cold.'

'This business of behaving like a gentleman and pretending to believe a lady, no matter what story she tells, is a great impediment to rational argument. *I* did not find it cool. The dozen or more ladies sitting at those tables were not shivering. I am left to conclude that you suffer from a unique malady – cold blood.'

'Surely sangfroid is second nature to us English,' I said.

'A clever trick, ma'am. One would think you were trained in philosophy – or politics – but the cool blood blamed on us by the French has a quite different meaning, I believe. Whatever we discover about our relatives, it will remain *entre nous*. There is no reason that either family need suffer for wrongdoing on the part of now dead relatives.'

'Let us hope Steptoe can be induced to follow that gentlemanly sentiment.'

'Steptoe would sell his soul – for the right price. I see you gathering up your shawl and reticule. Don't forget this.' He handed me the ivory miniature, and I put it in my reticule.

Weylin assisted me with my shawl, and we went together to the bottom of the stairs, arm in arm, as comfortably as an old married couple. He did not accompany me abovestairs. I peered down from the landing and saw that he did not head back to his private parlour, but went outside again, probably back to the band concert to flirt with the ladies there. I did not think Lord Weylin needed any poetical reminding to gather his rosebuds while he may – but perhaps I should heed the lesson.

Chapter Ten

$\mathcal{M}$ama was asleep when I returned to our room. I undressed in the dark and went immediately to bed. She was up before me in the morning, after her long night's rest. When I opened my eyes, she was sitting in the dark, fully dressed, peering out at the road through a crack in the curtains.

'You are finally awake, Zoie. It is past eight o'clock. I am dying for a cup of tea, but did not like to disturb you by calling for a servant.'

'You need not have worried about that, Mama. We are to meet Lord Weylin in his parlour for breakfast. Why do you not go down now, if you want your tea?'

'I would feel uncomfortable alone with him,' she said.

'I doubt he will be there yet.'

'Did you stay out late last night?' she asked suspiciously. 'Not too late, I hope?'

'I did not; I expect Lord Weylin had a later night.'

The desire for tea overcame her native shyness of our host, and she ventured forth without me. When I had dressed and went below, I found her chatting to Lord Weylin as comfortably as if they were old friends.

'And that is how I came to recognize Lady Margaret in the

picture,' she was saying. She turned to me when I entered and said, 'Zoie! You did not tell me Lord Weylin was asking about my having seen Lady Margaret when she was young.'

'Surely you did not know her before she came to Parham?'

Weylin rose and bowed. I nodded, waiting for Mama's reply.

'I did not know her, exactly, but I had seen her. She was visiting the Blessingtons in Ireland one spring. I used to see her driving around in a dashing landau. She went to one or two of our assemblies, but stuck very much to her own set. I was never presented to her, and that is why I did not call on her at Parham, or expect her to call on me. She was just one of the sights people discussed that summer, like Farmer Dooley's five-legged calf, or a hanging at the crossroads.' Weylin's brows arched at these lowly comparisons. 'We thought her the most glamorous thing we had ever seen,' Mama assured him.

He drew my chair. When I was seated, he said, 'Your Uncle Barry was also in Ireland that summer. Your mama does not recall his ever having met Margaret.'

'It would not much surprise me if he had wangled it,' Mama said, 'for he was after the ladies something awful at that time. A regular flirt.'

'I fail to see how there could have been anything between them,' Weylin said. 'My aunt came back to England in the autumn, and married David MacIntosh. He carried her off to Scotland. She never returned until David died, ten years ago.'

Mama said, 'Barry set out for India that August, shortly before Lady Margaret left.'

'Then if they ever did meet,' I said, 'it seems it was no more than a brief encounter.'

We ordered breakfast, and while we ate, Lord Weylin said that his groom had returned with my sketchpad. I told Mama that I was to attempt a sketch of Lady Margaret as she looked when I knew her.

She nodded and threw in a new twist. 'You are assuming, then, that she and Barry did not wear a disguise here at Tunbridge. As they were so hell-bent on deceiving everyone, it seems to me they would have taken that elementary precaution.'

This added a whole new layer of difficulty to the problem. When breakfast was cleared away, Lord Weylin placed my sketchpad on the table and opened it at a drawing of Uncle Barry. 'Shall I draw in a mustache and beard?' I suggested. 'There are six drawings of him in this pad, so we could try different ways he might have changed his looks. Glasses, perhaps . . .'

'Why do you not let Lord Weylin do that, while you get on with sketching Lady Margaret, Zoie?' Mama suggested.

Weylin demurred, but was talked into trying his hand at adding the hirsute decorations while I aged Lady Margaret. First I did an enlargement of the ivory miniature. When I was satisfied with it, I examined Mama's face, to see the effect of advancing years. Gravity had drawn the skin down into pouches at the corner of her jaws. The lips had lost their fullness, and assumed a querulous downturn. I made these changes, glancing from time to time at Mama as I worked.

'Why do you keep looking at me, Zoie?' she demanded. 'I see what you are up to, using me as a model of old age. I am considerably younger than Lady Margaret was. And I have not fallen into flesh either.'

Mama can become quite testy when she is annoyed. I let off using her as a model and sketched from memory. Her next complaint was that she felt she ought to be doing something, when we were both so busy. 'I shall run up and get my embroidery,' she decided.

Weylin offered to send a servant. I also offered to go.

'I shall go myself. I am still good for something,' she said, and left.

Weylin glanced up and smiled an understanding smile. 'I wonder if we shall become crotchety when we are her age.'

'Mama is just bored. She likes to keep busy.'

'I see by your sketchpad that you keep busy as well, Miss Barron. I am impressed with these sketches. I looked through the book when the footman delivered it this morning. I hope you don't mind?'

'Not at all. This is only a rough sketchbook. My finished works are better, I hope.'

'I should like to see them sometime. You have a talent for catching the character of your sitter.'

'Thank you. I always preferred to draw people. I thought I had a bit of a knack for reading their characters, but I own I never fathomed my uncle's double life. Of course, we have only Steptoe's word for it that he was up to any tricks here.'

He put his pencil down and passed the sketchpad along to me. 'How is this?' he asked. He had drawn in a long, curled mustache and a spade beard, of the sort schoolboys use to deface public broadsheets.

A bubble of laughter erupted at the childish manner of his execution. 'Do you not feel you should put horns on his head, and a spear in his hand? This looks like Old Nick.'

'I told you I would be no good at this!'

I turned the page to another drawing of my uncle, and shaded in a small brush moustache and a short beard, of the sort an elderly gentleman might actually wear. 'Something like this was what I had in mind.'

Weylin studied it a moment in an approving manner. 'That certainly changes his appearance. I would hardly recognize him as the same man.'

'He might have worn glasses, too. Even green glasses.'

I turned the page and drew steel-rimmed glasses on the next

sketch. The change was less striking. I filled the glasses in with shadow, which concealed the eyes and made Barry less easily recognizable. Weylin stationed himself behind me while I finished off the ageing of Lady Margaret. It was distracting to have such a close observer, but his aunt was certainly recognizable from the final sketch.

'Amazing!' he said, sliding into the chair at my elbow. 'There is just one thing that puzzles me, Miss Barron.'

'What is that?'

'Why the deuce do you bother taking lessons from Borsini, when you are head and shoulders above him?'

The name Borsini was enough to throw me into a pelter, but the compliment did much to mitigate it. 'I have learned a great deal from him,' I replied. 'Not just in executing art, but in appreciating the great artists of history. Sometimes he brings art books with him, and explains the work of the masters. He is very familiar with all the great works in Italy, of course.'

Weylin's lips stretched into a grin. 'I have heard before that it is not the painting lessons *per se* that are his chief attraction. I daresay some ladies go for that foreign strain.'

'I am interested in art, milord, not dalliance,' I said, and examined my conscience to see if it was true.

I had not learned much about painting techniques from Borsini for the past year. More and more the 'lessons' involved examining the works of the Renaissance masters, as we sat with our heads together, while he related tales, probably apocryphal, of the great Italian homes where he ran tame. I had to wonder why he had left Italy, for he obviously did not enjoy the patronage of the nobility in England. Yet to think of painting in solitude in my new octagonal studio was less pleasant than to think of being there with Borsini. Had I been hiring a gigolo, and not a painting teacher? No, he always behaved beautifully. He was more like a brother than a flirt. Oh, he took note of my gowns and coiffures and so on, but that was the art critic coming out in him.

'And Borsini? What is his main interest?' Weylin asked.

I felt it was the fee he was paid, but of course, did not say so. Instead I said, 'Can you think of any way your aunt might have changed her appearance? Obviously a moustache or beard are ineligible, unless she was posing as a man.'

Weylin chewed a smile. 'I hardly think so.' I should mention that his aunt's excess flesh had gone mostly to her bosom and hips. One could only laugh to think of so much femininity stuffed into trousers.

Mama came down with her embroidery just as the sketching was finished. Weylin said, 'Will you come with us on this search, Mrs Barron, or would you prefer the comfort of the parlour? Our morning will involve a deal of walking. Perhaps you would be more comfortable here with your embroidery.'

I felt his solicitude was a pretext to be rid of her, so that we two might have an unexceptionable excuse to spend the morning alone together, and was not entirely happy when Mama replied, 'I am bored to flinders sitting on my haunches. I shall go with you. Why do you not take your aunt's picture and show it about, milord, while we take Barry's? In that way, we shall cover the ground twice as quickly.'

'But . . .' He wanted to object, but could find no fault with such a sensible suggestion.

'An excellent idea, Mama,' I said.

Weylin rolled his aunt's sketch into a tube and left, after arranging to meet us back here for lunch.

As soon as he was gone, Mama said, 'We would not want him listening if we learn anything to Barry's discredit. I had a reason for suggesting he might have been in disguise, Zoie.' My heart sank. 'When I was searching out a clean shirt to bury him in, I found a clerical collar in his drawer – and a false moustache. You recall he had that old black suit he never wore. I happened to notice once when I was just tidying his room while he was in London that he had taken it with him. I hoped he was not trying to pass it off as a formal suit, for it was the wrong cut.'

'Good lord! Why did you not tell me?'

'It did not seem important – until now.'

'I had best alter another of the sketches,' I said, and drew in a clerical collar and moustache, before we went out to begin canvassing the hotels and jewelry stores.

We had no luck tracing Barry at any of the larger hotels. The Calverley, the Mount Pleasant, Earl's Court, the Royal Mount Ephraim, the Carlton, the Swan, the Camden – none of them recognized him in any of his guises. We took all the sketches with us. In moustache or beard, in green glasses or in clerical garb, he was unknown. That left dozens of small, private hotels.

'Let us try some jewelry shops,' I said, expecting the same result.

Our first stop was a small, dingy place behind the colonnade, with the unlikely name Kashmir, Prop. Albert Bradford. We thought the sequestered location and Indian name might have enticed Barry. We had perfected our technique by that time, omitting the use of a name fot Barry. I opened the sketchpad to the clerical likeness of my uncle and held it up. 'I am trying to locate an old relative. He is interested in jewelry. I just wondered if he had ever come in here.'

The man behind the counter had a small magnifying glass attached to his head by a band that held it over one eye. He lifted the glass and glanced at the picture. The man was older than Barry, about seventy, to judge by his grey hair and lined face. He had bright brown eyes and a ready smile.

'Ah, you're friends of Reverend Portland,' he said, and offered his hand. 'I am Albert Bradford. I haven't seen the reverend lately. Not ill, I hope?'

Mama and I exchanged a startled glance. We had not foreseen this question, and hardly knew how to reply. I said, 'I hope not. As I mentioned, we are just trying to locate Reverend Portland.'

'I have not seen him for months. He was used to drop in regularly to sell the jewelry his uncle left him. You would know about the jewelry, of course?'

We were highly desirous of hearing it. 'About India, you mean?' Mama ventured.

Albert Bradford nodded. 'The old nabob uncle who left him a small fortune in jewelry. There is no place like India for making your fortune. I was there myself, as you might have suspected from the name of my shop. I came home with a purseful of unmounted gemstones. My first thought was to sell them to a gems merchant, but I soon realized the real profit is in selling jewelry, so I had them made up by a jeweler I know. He is teaching me the trade.'

'Did Reverend Portland sell you much jewelry?' I asked.

'Not a great deal. About fifteen thousand it would come to, in all. The emerald necklace was the best of the lot.'

Mama looked as if she had been shot with an arrow. I knew exactly what she was thinking. Barry had turned thief, and had sold his ill-gotten gains to this unsuspecting man.

I swallowed and said, 'Was this recently? I mean did he sell you the jewelry all at one time, or—'

'Oh no, just as he needed the blunt, you know. Our clerics are not well paid. He first came into my shop about five years ago, to sell a diamond tie pin. A dandy piece, a flawless diamond. I had it mounted in a ring and sold it to Lady Montague. I told the reverend if he had any more such items, I would be happy to buy them. He was back in six months with a sapphire ring, then the next time with a ruby brooch.'

'Did he ever sell a diamond necklace?' I asked, thinking of Lady Margaret's necklace.

He pondered a moment, then said, 'Not a diamond necklace, no. Was he some kin to you, ladies?'

'A cousin,' I said. 'We are from out of town, actually. We are trying to trace Cousin Portland. Someone reported having seen him hereabouts. You would not know where he lived?'

'I know it was not right in town,' Bradford replied promptly. 'He had a little cottage in the countryside, down toward Ashdown Forest. I was never there myself. He always brought his pieces to me.'

'You would not have his address in your account book?' Mama asked. 'We are so very anxious to find him,' she added, with a sweet smile that would fool Satan himself.

'I don't,' Bradford answered. 'The reverend was a secretive sort of a fellow. I do not mean sly. Pray do not think I am disparaging him. It is just that he kept pretty well to business. If he had not been a man of the cloth, I would have suspected where he was getting all those fine pieces,' he added with a laugh. 'But when I dropped him a hint, he told me about his nabob uncle.'

'Uncle Barry.' Mama nodded.

'I don't believe he ever mentioned the name. I know from experience that many a fine piece comes from India. If you find your cousin, ladies, tell him I am still open for business.'

'Thank you,' I said, and snatched up my sketchpad. We escaped into the street, trembling like aspens in a gale.

'He was a thief!' Mama gasped. 'I am so glad Lord Weylin was not with us.'

'At least he did not steal Lady Margaret's necklace.'

'He did not sell it to that nice Mr Bradford,' Mama countered, 'but that is not to say he did not steal it. He knew she came to Tunbridge, you see, so he would have got rid of her necklace farther away, in London, very likely. I must be grateful he did not help himself to my poor chips of sapphire, that your papa gave me as a wedding gift.'

'We had best get back to the hotel. It is nearly time for lunch,' I said, drawing out my watch to check the time.

'What shall we tell him?' Mama asked, in a frightened way. She meant, of course, Lord Weylin.

'Nothing. We had no luck in finding Uncle Barry.'

'I wonder if he discovered anything of his aunt.'

We headed back to the hotel, with our heads low, scheming how to hide our disgrace. 'We ought to rush straight back to Hernefield, and take these sketches with us,' Mama said.

'I should like to make a detour to Ashdown Forest, and see if we can find any trace of Reverend Portland first.'

'Impersonating a minister! That was really too bad of Barry. But not so bad as stealing all that jewelry. ' She came to a dead stop. 'Zoie! Our wits have gone begging! The money he got from Bradford must be in his house at Ashdown Forest – if he actually had such a house. That might be more lies.'

'We have found no trace of him at any of the local hotels. It is worth a try.'

'We shall go as soon as we can be rid of Weylin,' Mama declared.

When this was settled, we continued on our way back to the hotel, and lunch with Lord Weylin.

Chapter Eleven

Lord Weylin had not returned to the hotel when we arrived. We went abovestairs to tidy up for luncheon, and make further plans to delude him. I was sorry to cut Weylin out of our adventure. It was not every day such an eligible gentleman crossed my path. Mama had warned me against setting my cap for him; indeed I knew myself he was above my touch, but common sense never prevented a lady from hoping. If he was interested in me, there was nothing to prevent him from following up the acquaintance after we got back to Hernefield. He had said he wished to see my paintings.

Weylin had still not returned when we went downstairs. It was well past the time we had agreed to meet. His tardiness suggested he had found some clue that he was following up. We inquired at the desk whether he had left a message.

The clerk handed me a note. 'It is not from his lordship. This arrived with the noon mail,' he said. I recognized Brodagan's broad fist. Mama and I took it to the parlour.

'This will be some tale of woe. Brodagan and Steptoe have come to cuffs very likely,' Mama said, ripping the note open. She glanced at it, gave an angry *tsk*, and handed it to me.

With amendments to spelling for your convenience, this is what I read:

Steptoe has upped and gone with never a word to a soul. His head never dented his pillow last night, for I used my key when he did not come down this morning and saw it for myself. The creature was still here when Lord Weylin's footman stopped for milady's book of pictures. Steptoe was quizzing the lad at the doorway. It would not surprise me if he has lit out for Tunbridge to do you a mischief. A look before you is better than two behind, milady. Mrs Chawton has been hounding us to death to know about the Book Society. Mary has got a boil on her nose and looks like a witch. Your servant, Mrs Brodagan.

'Steptoe!' I said. 'Now what can he be up to?'

'No good – that is certain,' Mama replied. 'We must keep an eye peeled for him.'

When Lord Weylin had still not returned ten minutes later, we ordered wine to pass the time. No sooner was it poured than he came rushing in, full of apologies.

'Did you find any trace of Lady Margaret?' I asked.

He shook his head. 'I have been at every hotel in town, public and private. It is a complete mystery to me where she stayed. I begin to think she had a fellow in London, and was pulling the wool over our eyes with her tale of coming to Tunbridge Wells. Did you ladies have any luck?'

'No,' we replied in unison, with suspicious alacrity.

I feared Weylin would notice our wary manner, but he was distracted. It was not long in dawning on me that he was concealing a secret himself. His manner was too hearty and his avowals of how hard he had looked were too strong not to cause suspicion. I feared he had learned Barry's secret, and was trying to hide it from us. If he had made inquiries at the Kashmir Jewelry Shop, for instance, Bradford might have said, 'That is odd. I had two ladies in looking for their cousin this very morning.' Our description would leave Weylin in little doubt who the ladies were. But why keep it from us? Was it gentlemanly concern for our feelings, or was his reason darker?

We ordered lunch, and while we ate, I asked nonchalantly, 'Did you go to any jewelry shops, milord, or only to hotels?'

His head jerked up. 'Jewelry stores? No. Why do you ask?'

He had certainly been to jewelry stores. 'Because of your aunt's missing necklace,' I replied with an innocent stare.

'No, there was not time. The best course is for me to make a few inquiries in London. It seems my aunt was not coming to Tunbridge all these years at all. Are you ladies about ready to throw in the towel? I fear it is a hopeless case.'

Mama relaxed into a smile of relief. 'We were thinking we might as well be getting on home, too,' she said.

'Very wise. We are hunting for a mare's nest. It was foolish to think we could discover anything at this late date.'

Once it was established we were all leaving Tunbridge, Lord Weylin became quite merry. It was obvious he wanted to get away from us as much as we wanted to be rid of him.

'In fact,' he said, 'I see no reason to waste a whole afternoon. I shall set out for London right after lunch.'

'We might as well go home, too,' Mama said. I agreed, but said I would visit the shops first, to make it sound casual.

Weylin was on his feet without even waiting for dessert. 'I shall settle up the bill here and be on my way, then. I shall ask them to keep the parlour for your use until you leave. You might want tea after raiding the shops, Miss Barron.'

'Let us split the bill,' Mama said. 'We have had more use of the parlour than you. There are two of us.'

He lifted his hand in a peremptory way. 'Allow me.'

'We must pay for our own mutton at least,' Mama insisted.

'You have been an inestimable help. May I call on you when I return?' He looked at me and continued, 'You were kind enough to say I might see some of your paintings, Miss Barron.'

'We shall be happy to see you, milord,' I replied.

Mama reminded him of the notice he was to put in the journals, asking if anyone had seen his aunt.

'I forgot to do it. No point now,' Weylin said. That suggested to me that he already had a line on her. 'I look forward to seeing you at Hernefield in a day or two. Ladies.' He bowed and scurried out the door as if chased by a bear.

Mama clapped her hands together and laughed. 'There is one stroke of luck. We shan't have to worry about Weylin finding out about Barry. I doubt he will learn much in London.'

'Let us give him half an hour to get on his way before we go to Ashdown Forest,' I said, and poured another cup of tea.

'What about Steptoe?' Mama asked. 'One of us should remain here to keep an eye out for him.'

'If he shows up, he should be followed,' I agreed, 'but do you not think it more likely he is here to follow us?'

'It is not certain he is here at all. He may have taken advantage of our absence to go off to a horse-race or dogfight. Still, I think I should remain behind, Zoie. I shall stay at the hotel for an hour, then take a stroll along the Pantiles and look about for him.'

'I am the one who should stay, Mama. You could not keep up with the weasel if it comes to following him on foot.'

'You would be mistaken for a lightskirt if you were to dawdle about the colonnade alone. No, I shall stay, and you take the carriage to Ashdown Forest to inquire after Reverend Portland,' she said, giving the alias a disdainful accent.

That is what we did. I took the sketch of Barry disguised as a minister. The road to Ashdown Forest led through a well-wooded weald, the remains of the immense oak forest that once provided the best oak timber for building ships. While the carriage clipped along, I mentally arranged my plans. I would stop at the post office to inquire for Reverend Portland's address. If Uncle had bought the cottage he lived in, then presumably it now stood empty, for it was not mentioned in his Will. I would get Rafferty, our groom, to help me break in and search the place for clues, if it was in a secluded location. If Uncle had only hired the cottage, then perhaps the new occupants or the neighbors could tell me something about him.

The main road through the area was called Forest Row. It had scattered houses, mostly of timber, and an occasional church or school. We stopped at a few houses; I inquired for the Reverend Portland, showing the sketch. In each case, I received a disinterested shake of the head. No one had ever seen or heard of him. The last dame was kind enough to direct me to the closest post office, at West Hoathly. We continued and found the village, which stood on a hilltop above Ashdown Forest, but the name Reverend Portland was not known at the post office. The clerk suggested we try Lindfield, which he assured us we had already passed.

The carriage was turned around, we retraced our steps, and did indeed discover a village called Lindfield. We had not spotted the High Street from the path, but it was picturesque, with elegant Tudor and Georgian houses. I made one last try at the post office there. I could not remember Mr Bradford's exact words, but he had said my uncle's cottage was in the countryside, near Ashdown Forest, or something of the sort. I pulled the check string, and Rafferty drew to a stop. When he let down the step for me, he wore a frown. Rafferty, I should explain, is an old and trusted servant, of the sort called black Irish. His hair was once black, and his eyes are still a beautiful blue. He came from Ireland twenty years ago as a lad, and is practically family. He did not know the precise reason for our trip, but he knew something havey-cavey was afoot.

'I see Lord Weylin's rig is parked down the street,' he said. 'That is odd. His groom mentioned he was off to London.'

'Weylin is here! Good God! Get back on your perch and get us out of here at once, Rafferty, before he sees us.'

Rafferty is amazingly spry for his years. Before you could blink, the carriage was rattling around the corner. He drove several yards down the side road before stopping. I did not wait for him to open the door, but bolted out to spy on Weylin from behind the tree closest to his carriage.

'I shall be back shortly,' I said, and ran off.

I was just in time to see Weylin enter his carriage and drive away. I could see only one explanation for his being here. He had spoken to Bradford and learned about Barry selling what must surely be stolen jewelry. He was checking up on him behind our backs. As he was at such pains to deceive us, he obviously intended to prosecute, if it is possible to prosecute the relatives of a felon. In any case, he hoped to prove Barry had stolen the neck-lace and shame us into paying for it. Why else was he going to such pains to trace Barry's movements?

Between fear and anger, I was trembling all over when Rafferty caught up with me. 'Shall I follow him?' he asked.

'No, I shall stop at the post office while we are here, and have a look at that house Weylin came out of, too.'

The post office was run by an elderly married couple, the Sangsters. They were both small and greyhaired, with the quick, twitchy manner of mice. The man was sorting the mail, while his wife tended to customers. I waited until the last one left before inquiring if she knew the address of Reverend Portland. She did not, but her little nose twitched in curiosity. I unrolled the sketch and showed it to her.

She shook her head. 'No dear. I've never seen him. Vicar Quarles has been here for two decades.'

'Are there other post offices in nearby villages?' I asked. 'I am very eager to find Reverend Portland. His late sister was my mother's friend. The sister recently passed away, and we want to let him know,' I said, to distance myself from Barry, in case he was a known felon in these parts.

'Now, that is odd!' she exclaimed. 'This seems to be a day for lost relatives – and for bringing a sketch along, too. So very odd, for it has never happened before. I had a gentleman in not twenty minutes ago looking for his long-lost cousin. He had her picture with him, too. He did not even know her name, for he heard she had married since he last saw her. He was a lord,' she said, lifting her eyebrows into her hairline. 'His carriage had a lozenge on the door. I was sorry to have to tell him his cousin was dead. She was used to come here often before she died, but I do not know Reverend Portland.' Her head ducked forward in concern. 'Are you feeling weak, dear? Let me get you a glass of water. You look pale as a sheet.'

She darted off for water, while I sank against the counter. Weylin had shown Mrs Sangster my sketch of Lady Margaret, and the woman had recognized her! Lady Margaret had been here, in that house that Weylin was coming out of. At least he had not discovered that Barry also lived nearby.

Mrs Sangster returned with the water. I sipped it slowly, while trying to think how I could elicit more information from her without arousing too much curiosity. She was inclined to gossip, and I said, 'I believe I saw that lord's carriage – the one who was looking for his cousin. It was halted just a few yards along the street.'

'At his cousin's house. I pointed it out to him. Mrs Langtree's house,' she said. 'She was ever so nice. A real lady, but retiring. She did not go out much. Of course, she was only here a few times a year. Her home is in London. She came to get away from the bustle for a week or so every season.'

'Did she come here all alone?' I asked.

Had Mrs Sangster been a suspicious sort, she must have wondered at such an odd question. Fortunately, she was more interested in gossip than anything else, and answered readily.

'Oh no! She had her woman with her. Ladies of quality would not travel alone. She had that nice young nephew who used to stay with her as well, Mr Jones. And a male servant, too. Real quality. She was ever so fond of Mr Jones.'

It was the word 'nephew' that brought Weylin to mind, but a second thought told me he was not Mr Jones, or the postmistress would have recognized him. Who could Mr Jones be?

'Who is living in the house now?' I asked.

'No one. Mr Jones inherited the house. He would have no use for it, which is why he has put it up for sale.'

'Ah! It is for sale.' So perhaps Weylin had not actually got inside, but had just had a look. I had only seen him coming away from it. I knew at once how I could get into the house, though what I hoped to find was unclear.

'The estate agent is Mr Folyot. He has his office just at the end of High Street,' Mrs Sangster said.

I was eager to call on Mr Folyot, and said, 'I shan't take up more of your time, Mrs Sangster. Thank you very much.'

'Sorry I could not help you, Miss. . . ?'

'Smith. Miss Smith,' I replied, and escaped.

I could not like to give my own name. Smith, the most

common name in the country, popped out without thinking. Smith or Jones are the usual aliases. I thought of Mr Jones, and wondered, was that also an alias?

I had Rafferty drive by the house Weylin had been coming out of. It was only a cottage, but a pretty one in the Tudor style, with plaster and half timber on the top floor, and brickwork below. There was a FOR SALE sign posted. The windows were boarded up. I pulled the check string, and Rafferty drew to a stop. I peered out at overgrown grass. Well-tended roses along the border of the walk spoke of recent habitation.

While I was looking from the carriage window, a man came walking along and turned in at the house. The stuffed shoulders and pinched waist of his jacket indicated a lack of gentility. He wore his hat at a cocky angle, and had the strut of a man who thinks well of himself. He was actually holding a brass key in his hand. Mr Folyot! I leapt out and accosted him.

'Are you the agent for this house?' I asked.

A pair of sharp, green eyes smiled at me. 'That I am, madam. Are you on the lookout for a cottage hereabouts?'

'Indeed I am. Could I have a look at the inside?'

'Why not? I am about to go in and have a look around myself. You will find it a nice, snug place. The present owner had it done up over five years ago.'

He unlocked the door and stepped into a perfectly dark house. 'I shall just light a few lamps. I had the windows boarded up to prevent vandalism,' he explained.

When the lamps were lit, I peered around at an elegant hallway, still very dark due to the wood paneling. He led me through the saloon and dining room and library, pointing out the desirable features of the house. I had to take his word for it that the furnishings, included in the sale price, were of the quality he described, for I could scarcely see them in the gloom. My real interest was not in the house or furnishings, but anything that might suggest my uncle had been here. After touring below, we went upstairs. All personal items had been removed. There was nothing to indicate habitation by Lady Margaret or anyone else. The dresser tops were bare, the clothes presses empty. The mysterious 'nephew' must have tidied up. 'Very nice,' I said to Folyot from time to time.

'Mind you don't delay too long if you're interested in buying, Miss Smith.' I was still, or again, Miss Smith. 'I have another fellow coming to look at the house this very afternoon, which is why you found me here. Ah! That will be Mr Welland now,' he said, when the door knocker sounded. He hastened along to the front door.

I had a horrible premonition who Mr Welland would be. And indeed it was none other than Lord Weylin. It would be hard to say which of us was more shocked and embarrassed. We exchanged a long, silent look as Mr Folyot introduced us.

'How do you do, Miss Smith,' Lord Weylin said in perfectly wooden accents.

'Good day, Mr Welland,' I replied, and dashed out the door, with Folyot hollering after me that he would he happy to have the boards taken down to give me a better look, if I thought the house would suit me.

'Thank you. I shall let you know,' I said, and ran to the carriage. 'Spring 'em,' I called to Rafferty.

'Back to the hotel, Miss Barron?'

'Yes, as fast as you can go.'

The whip snapped, and I was tossed around the seat like a pig in a poke all the way to Tunbridge Wells.

Chapter Twelve

*I*n the depths of my embarrassment, the only thing I could
think of was running away and hiding. Mama would have to
sell Hernefield and move back to Ireland, where we would never
have to face Lord Weylin again. He knew my uncle was a thief,
that he had stolen Lady Margaret's necklace and a great deal more.
When I emptied my budget to Mama back at the hotel, she was
no more optimistic than myself, but more curious.

'What on earth was Lady Margaret doing at Lindfield?' she
kept asking. 'And with a young fellow, you say?'

'A Mr Jones. She was calling herself Mrs Langtree. Barry must
have tumbled to it that she was up to something, and been holding her to ransom. As his thievery was never reported, at least to
our knowledge, it stands to reason he was not only a thief, but
worse. He ferreted out his victims' secrets and made them pay
him to keep mum. I daresay Mr Jones was the secret.'

'Do you think he was Lady Margaret's . . . paramour?' she said,
blurting the last word out in an explosion of distaste.

A little smile seized my lips at having found some disrepute in
Weylin's family to dilute the shame of my own. 'Mrs Sangster did
say Mrs Langtree was ever so fond of Mr Jones. The name sounds
like an alias.'

'And she left him the cottage as well. She would not do that for no reason. The old fool took a lover half her age. Well, there is no accounting for taste.'

'That was certainly foolish, but it is not indictable. We are in the worse pickle, Mama. What should we do?'

'Go home.'

I wanted to, but that was a craven impulse. 'If we could find Barry's money, we could pay Weylin for the necklace without mortgaging Hernefield. We must stay and try to find where he lived. Bradford said he had a cottage near Ashdown Forest. There are dozens of little villages tucked away there.'

'I wager Steptoe knows more than he is telling,' Mama said. 'I think it is time to bargain with him, Zoie. Oh, did I tell you he is here, in Tunbridge? I spotted him on the Pantiles this afternoon. I tried to follow him, but he moved like greased lightning. I think he was looking for us, for he popped into half a dozen hotels, and right back out again.'

'He did not see you, then?'

'No, but he probably knows by now where we are staying.'

'Then we have only to sit tight and he will call.'

At that precise moment, a sharp rap came at our door. We both jumped an inch from our seats. I rose and strode to the door, wearing my sternest face to frighten Steptoe, flung the door open, and found myself staring at Lord Weylin.

'May I come in?' he asked, and walked past me into the room, before I had the wits to bar the door.

'Oh, you are still here, Lord Weylin,' Mama said. Her face was cherry red with shame.

'Did your daughter not tell you we met at Lindfield?' he replied mildly.

There was something very much amiss with this visit. Weylin should have come in like a lion, snarling and gnashing his teeth.

His manner had a definite aroma of the sheep.

'Pray be seated, milord,' I said, but as I looked about the room, it became clear that if he took the other chair, I must either stand or stretch myself out on the bed.

'I came to invite you ladies to join me for tea, as we have all decided to remain another day and continue looking for our shameless relatives. Not that I mean to cast aspersions on Mr McShane's character,' he added hastily.

This became stranger by the moment. 'Mama?' I said.

'I could do with a cup of tea,' she replied.

Weylin accompanied us to the same parlour as before, leaving no opportunity for private discussion between Mama and myself, but mother and daughter do not necessarily require words to communicate. We both realized that Weylin was on the hot seat, and were on nettles to discover why.

He ordered a lavish tea, with enough sandwiches and sweets to feed a parish. He could not have been more attentive to our comfort if we had been a pair of duchesses. Chairs were drawn, and discarded due to an imaginary draft. Shawls were arranged, and at one point he even suggested we remove to a larger parlour. During these ludicrous goings-on, he kept flashing quick looks at me, as if to see whether I meant to attack him.

When he tried to change my chair for the second time, my curiosity could endure no more. 'For God's sake, Weylin, what have you discovered?' I demanded. It was the first time I had dispensed with his title when speaking to him. I felt a little forward, but if he noticed, he was too shaken to show it.

His brows rose in a question. 'Why, exactly what you discovered yourself, I should think. My foolish aunt had taken herself a young lover, and handed her diamond necklace over to him. Not only her necklace, but whatever monies she had. You are not privy to all the details of her Will, ladies. The fact is, MacIntosh left her a hefty fortune, which I understood was destined for myself. At her death, it was completely gone. Vanished – along with the necklace.'

Mama and I executed one of those tacit communications. I nodded my consent, and she said, 'We were wondering if Mr Jones might be her paramour.' Mama disliked to use the word 'lover' but I think 'paramour' was no better. It has a shady sound to it.

'I do not see what else he could be.' Weylin scowled. 'The post-mistress was quite forthcoming about how fond she was of the fellow. Buying him a gig and watches and I don't know what all. I am sorry I implied your uncle was involved in the theft of the necklace – but it is odd he ended up with the copy.'

'What led you to Lindfield, Lord Weylin?' I asked.

'I assume it is the same thing that led you there. I noted your question, at lunch, as to whether I had visited any jewelry shops. I also noticed you did not believe me when I told a bald lie. I hope you can forgive me. It is extremely distasteful to admit one's aunt was such a fool, and a lecher, too, at her age. I hoped to keep it from you. I learned in Krupps Jewelry Shop that my aunt had sold her necklace. I told the jeweler my cousin had married, and I was unaware of her married name, but he recognized your sketch, Miss Barron. She used the name Mrs Langtree. The address she gave was Lindfield. The postmistress there directed me to the house.'

I wondered at her selling the necklace herself, and soon figured out that Barry had demanded cash, which occasioned the sale.

'Perhaps you are too hard on her, milord,' Mama said. 'She might have married Jones, for all we know to the contrary.'

'That is hardly an improvement, in my opinion!' he said.

We sat with our tongues between our teeth, not revealing by so much as a blink that we were already aware of this story, and certainly not intimating that Barry had been up to tricks of his own. But we were keenly aware of it, and it was this that softened our condemnation of Lady Margaret. She may have been a fool, but at least she was not a thief.

'There is really nothing to keep me in Tunbridge Wells now,' Weylin said. 'I got the address of Jones's man of business from Folyot, the estate agent at Lindfield. I mean to find out Jones's address and call on him in London to rattle a few sabres. If he actually married my aunt, of course, there is little that can be done to recover her fortune, but if he was only her lover . . . well, her Will left her entire estate to me.'

'Then how did Jones get his hands on it?' I asked. 'Mrs Sangster said Mr Jones had inherited the house.'

'Yes, from Mrs Langtree,' Weylin pointed out, with a tight smile. 'She was not Mrs Langtree, but Lady Margaret MacIntosh. Any lawyer worth his salt could undo such a Will with one hand behind his back. Much depends on what sort of fellow Jones is. If he is an out-and-out rotter – and really I do not see how he can be anything else – then I shall set the law after him. When a fellow in his twenties marries a lady nudging sixty, you may be sure it is not her *beaux yeux* he is after.'

'He was passing as her nephew,' I said. 'Is there such a relative in the family, even one with a different name?'

'No. I thought of that, of course. There is no nephew except myself. There is her stepson, MacIntosh's son by his first wife, but he is a carrot top. No one ever accused him of being handsome, and besides, he has his estate in Scotland. He has not been dashing off to Lindfield four times a year for the past five years. Old MacIntosh had no nephews. No, it is some scoundrel who preyed on Aunt Margaret's susceptibility for romance. She was always a fool for a handsome young man. But enough of my problems,' Weylin said. 'You have not had any luck in following Mr McShane's trail, I take it?'

'No. No, we have not,' Mama said warily.

Weylin said, 'I spotted Steptoe as I drove into the yard. As he was leaving this hotel, I assumed he had called on you.'

'He was here?' I asked, starting up from my chair.

Mama clutched her heart. 'It is odd he did not call on us,' she said. 'I wager we shall hear from him e'er long.'

Weylin drew out his watch and frowned at it. 'Since he bothered to follow you here, why did he not call? I begin to wonder if Steptoe knows as much as you think. His sly behavior suggests he is only trying to discover what is afoot himself.'

'He came to the wrong place then,' Mama said, 'for we do not know what is going on.'

Weylin kept his watch in the palm of his hand, glancing at it from time to time. 'Are you in a hurry to get to London, Lord Weylin? Pray, do not let us detain you,' I said.

'I was trying to decide whether to leave at once and make it before dark, or to remain overnight and leave first thing in the morning.' He returned the watch to his pocket and said, 'I shall stick around until morning. Mr Jones is not likely to disappear. He has no idea I am on to him. I could not get much of a look around my aunt's love nest with Folyot at my elbow. I mean to return after dark and break in.'

'What on earth for?' Mama demanded.

'My aunt's last illness came on suddenly. She had planned to return to the love nest. It stands to reason she must have left some personal items there. I shall root through the drawers to see if I can find anything to incriminate Jones.'

'Surely he would have checked himself before putting the house up for sale,' I said.

'He had no reason to fear I would tumble to his trick. Folyot said a local woman had tidied the place up, but she would not take it on herself to throw out letters and such things. I shall make a thorough search tonight.'

Mama cleared her throat and said, 'That would be against the law, would it not, Lord Weylin?'

'Yes, it would. I hope you are not planning to report me?'

'No indeed.'

We spoke of other things. Weylin kept returning to the riddle of how Barry came to have the copy of his aunt's necklace. His fear was that she had conned him into believing it was the original, and sold it to him at a criminally high price. At one point he even said he would repay us, if this turned out to be the case.

We parted the best of friends. We were all to regroup at the private parlour at seven-thirty for dinner, before Weylin left to break in to his late aunt's love nest. When Mama and I were back in our room, we agreed we would begin scouring the countryside around Ashdown Forest for Barry's cottage as soon as Weylin left for London in the morning. Meanwhile we had that dinner to look forward to. Weylin was in such a penitential mood that it promised to be an enjoyable repast.

Chapter Thirteen

Since the shroud had been such a success the evening before, I wore it again, with a different shawl to vary the look. Instead of my Grecian coiffure, I pulled my hair all to one side, fastened it with a clip, and let a cluster of curls hang flirtatiously down to my shoulder. The do had looked well in *La Belle Assemblée*, but when I examined myself in the mirror, I felt I should be simpering. There was something coy in that teasing curl on my shoulder. It looked feminine, however, and I wished to remind Weylin that I was a woman, as well as a lady. We were about to go down to the parlour when there was a discreet tap at the door.

'Weylin is early,' I said, hastening toward the door.

There stood Steptoe, with the slyest look you ever saw on his face. 'May I have a word with you, madam?' he asked.

'Why are you not at Hernefield, Steptoe?' I demanded.

'I thought you might require my services here, madam.'

'You are mistaken.'

'You are not looking for Mr McShane's residence in this neighborhood then, madam?' he asked, bold as brass.

I opened the door and let the wretched creature come in. Mama had recognized his voice and came forward, staring like a moonling. She did not say a word. I could not let him know we were

108

scared to death of what he might say. I said nonchalantly, while arranging my shawl, 'What do you have to tell us, Steptoe? Pray hurry. Lord Weylin is expecting us for dinner.'

'About my increase in salary, madam . . .'

'About Mr McShane's residence, Steptoe—' I replied.

'An increase of five pounds a quarter would suit me.'

'No doubt, but you are not earning it by vacating your post without permission, are you?'

'Five pounds, and I give you the name of the village,' he said, peering at me with his bold, snuff-brown eyes.

'For five pounds I will require not only the village, but the house.'

'Five pounds for the village, and that is my final offer.'

'Then you may go to the devil!'

'His lordship might be interested to hear about your uncle's criminal doings with young Jones,' he said, his smile stretching to a grin.

There was another tap at the door. We all three – Steptoe, Mama, and myself – froze. 'That will be Weylin!' I whispered.

'The clothespress!' Steptoe said, and darted into it while Mama and I stood gaping.

The tap came again. I swallowed the lump in my throat and went to answer it. It was Weylin.

He smiled and said, 'Very charming, Miss Barron,' while his eyes traveled over my face, lingering in an approving way at the cluster of curls hanging at my shoulder.

Mama came pelting forward and said, 'Let us go below. I am famished.' She herded Weylin out the door on a stream of chatter. 'I cannot imagine why, because I scarcely moved all day, and had that delicious tea. There is something about traveling that always makes one so hungry.'

We got Weylin away without his seeing Steptoe, but I was

extremely uneasy to think of that wretch alone in our room, pawing through our belongings. The dreadful word 'criminal doings' reeled in my head. I could see no solution but to give him the extra five pounds per quarter. We would be his banker for the rest of our mortal days.

As soon as the waiter arrived, I excused myself to dart upstairs. Steptoe would expect me to return, and be waiting.

'Just order whatever you are having for me, Mama,' I said, while the waiter poured wine and the others examined the menu. 'I have forgotten my handkerchief. I shan't be a moment.'

Weylin said, 'I have a handkerchief, Miss Barron, if—' He noticed my strained expression, and said no more. I think he assumed some feminine need, and was too gentlemanly to press the unwanted handkerchief on me.

I left and hastened up to our room. The lamps were still burning. 'You can come out, Steptoe. I am alone,' I called to the clothespress. There was no reply.

The door was ajar. I went and opened it. He was gone. I quickly checked my jewelry box. Mama's small diamond brooch and my pearl necklace were still there. I was about to leave when I espied a note stuck into my brush on the dresser. It said, 'Mr John Brown, Molyneux Park, 10:00 tonight.' Molyneux Park was a small private hotel catering to families and commercial travelers. John Brown presumably was Steptoe, and ten o'clock was the hour at which he would condescend to see us – but why did he use an alias?

I slipped the note into my reticule, wondering about that ominously vague 'criminal doings'. Bearing in mind our conversation with Bradford of the Kashmir Jewelry Shop, I could make an educated guess. I had an inkling what had happened to Barry's five thousand pounds, which so mysteriously disappeared as soon as he joined us at Hernefield. He had bought himself a cottage at some village near Tunbridge Wells, from which he conducted his criminal activities. Thank goodness he did not use Hernefield as his base of operation.

The only light in this dark tunnel was that such a thieving scoundrel must have his cottage stuffed full of money. Ill-gotten gains, to be sure, but the cottage at least belonged to him. Mama could sell it. We must try to learn the names of his victims, and return money equivalent to the value of what he had stolen. The future looked unpleasant, and over it all hung the menacing presence of Steptoe, who would bleed us dry.

I prepared a polite face and returned to the private parlour. Mama looked at me with blatant alarm. To allay her fears of imminent disaster, I said with a smile, 'Now I can enjoy dinner. What did you order for me, Mama?'

'Roast pork with prune sauce.'

'Lovely.'

Weylin said, 'We were just discussing Steptoe.'

I looked to see if Mama had revealed any secrets. She said hastily, 'We were wondering if he meant to be in touch with us, since Lord Weylin saw him near our hotel.'

'I expect we shall hear from him later this evening,' I said nonchalantly.

'Very likely,' Mama said, nodding her comprehension.

The meal progressed satisfactorily after that. Weylin joked about the broad criminal streak that ran in his family, with himself no better than he should be, what with breaking into a house that very night.

'Does that make us accessories?' I asked.

'Not unless you choose to come with me,' he said, with an inviting look.

I would have liked to go along, but of course, the meeting with Steptoe took precedence.

He continued his indirect persuasions. 'The house belongs to me, by rights. And even if I were caught, the fact that it was bought by my aunt would give some justification.'

'You need not worry on that score,' Mama said. She had obviously not figured out that he wanted me to accompany him. 'The law would never deal harshly with a lord.'

Weylin continued his inviting looks, but when I ignored them, he did not come right out and ask me. He promised to call and let us know what he discovered, if he was back by eleven. If he arrived later, he would meet us for breakfast in the morning. We did not linger after dinner. Weylin was eager to be off on his evening's romp. As soon as Mama and I were in our room, I handed her Steptoe's note.

She read it with a *tsk*. 'This wretched fellow will beggar us, Zoie. I don't know what Weylin will think when he learns the whole. I half wish we had told him. He was so forthcoming about his aunt's peccadilloes, he will think us sly.'

'Let us learn the whole truth from Steptoe before we confess. If Weylin recovers his aunt's fortune, he will be in a good mood. I own I do not like conning him.'

'He is much nicer than I thought. Quite human, really.'

'Yes, but not so nice as to continue friends with the relatives of thieves.'

We passed the time until our meeting in talking and looking at the journals. At a quarter to ten we called for the carriage and left for the Molyneux Park Hotel. It was a small, respectable place facing the Common. We inquired for Mr Brown and were directed to his room.

Steptoe answered the door promptly. 'Punctual!' he said, drawing out his watch. He held the door and we entered.

His condescending manner was enough to make me fly off the handle before I had even set foot in the room. It was a large,

112

comfortable room that he could certainly not afford on his butler's salary. A bottle of wine sat on the bedside table, with a cheroot in a dish beside it.

'We have no time to waste, Steptoe,' I said. 'If you know anything, tell us.'

'Five pounds,' he said.

Mama gave an angry tsk and said, 'Very well.'

Steptoe stuck his fingers in his vest, waited until he had our total attention, then announced, 'Lindfield.'

Mama and I exchanged a surprised look. 'Lindfield!' we both exclaimed together. Mama said, 'But that is where—'

'Never mind, Mama,' I said quickly, before she could say more. 'It is clear Steptoe knows nothing about this matter.'

'I saw Barry McShane in Lindfield on two occasions,' Steptoe said, coloring up in annoyance.

'Was he wearing a clerical collar?' Mama asked.

Steptoe took it for sarcasm and said, 'Certainly not! I tell you he was there. Once I followed him from Tunbridge, and once I went back when he said he was going to London, to check up on him. He went into a Tudor cottage on the High Street at ten o'clock at night, and did not come back out, though I waited for over two hours. It will be extra for the information on the house,' he said, when he realized what he had said. 'Our bargain was five pounds a quarter for the name of the village.'

I gave Mama a damping look, for she seemed on the verge of speech, and I did not wish her to reveal the significance of that Tudor house. 'Have you not heard, Steptoe?' I asked, smiling. 'Verbal contracts are not worth the air they are breathed on. Come along, Mama, we are wasting our time here. We shall expect you to be back at your post at Hernefield by noon tomorrow, or you will not receive any salary at all.'

'We had a bargain,' he said angrily.

'The bargain was that you would tell us what we wished to know. My uncle did not live in that cottage. We happen to be acquainted with the owner. You may have seen him visiting our friends. That is hardly worth twenty pounds a year for the rest of your life, is it?'

I rather wished I had said nothing, but Steptoe's blush suggested he thought he had made a fool of himself. 'What was the secret, then? He always let on he was going to London.' He thought a moment, then said, 'He had a ladybird?'

'What of it?' I asked airily. 'He was a bachelor, after all. The world will hardly condemn him for that. Let us go, Mama. Remember, Steptoe – noon tomorrow, or you may consider yourself dismissed.'

We scooted out the door before he could put two and two together – that Uncle had the copy of Lady Margaret's necklace, and the lady he was visiting was Lady Margaret. Apparently Steptoe had not spotted her.

Mama and I had a long discussion of all this after we returned to our hotel. 'I can see Barry visiting Lady Margaret,' Mama said, 'but staying two hours? That sounds like a friendly visit.'

'At ten o'clock in the evening, it sounds like a very friendly visit,' I agreed.

'Zoie, you are not suggesting that they were ... paramours? You are forgetting Mr Jones.'

'Perhaps she had a paramour for each day of the week,' I said, and collapsed in mirth on the bed. 'I wonder if Weylin will discover this secret when he breaks into the love nest.'

'I shall die of shame!'

'And so will he.'

Mama soon found new causes for worry. 'It still does not explain what he did with that missing five thousand pounds.'

114

'Perhaps he gave it to his light-o'-love – Lady Margaret.'

'The waste of it! And where did he get all that jewelry he was selling, and what was he doing with the paste necklace?'

'Perhaps the jewels all belonged to Lady Margaret, and he was selling them for her. Old MacIntosh was well to grass.'

'I daresay that could be the answer. And put on that clerical garb to fool Mr Bradford.'

'At least it has got Steptoe off our backs. How I enjoyed lighting into him.'

'I cannot get over the slyness of the pair of them. You would think Barry and Lady Margaret were strangers, to see them pass on the street with a nod, and all the while they were paramours. It is odd she would choose Barry when she has a colt's tooth in her head. I am thinking of Mr Jones.'

It was indeed odd, but I felt the mystery had been solved. Even my uncle's possession of the paste necklace was now comprehensible, if not entirely clear. If he sold her jewelry for her, it could have come into his possession in some harmless way. I was in a good mood when the servant brought a note to our room at ten past eleven.

'From Lord Weylin, madam,' the servant said. 'He said if your lights were out, not to disturb you. As I heard voices—'

'That is fine.' I glanced at the note, requesting us to go to the parlour if we were still dressed. 'You may tell Lord Weylin we shall be down presently.'

The servant left, and I said to Mama, 'Weylin is back, Mama. He wants to see us. This should be interesting.'

'You go, Zoie, and tell me what he has to say. I am ashamed to face him.'

'I cannot imagine why. It is his aunt who had the string of lovers. Barry is relatively innocent.'

'Aye, if we have heard the whole of it.'

'Goose!' I said, and gave her a kiss on the cheek before running downstairs to tease Lord Weylin.

Chapter Fourteen

I found Weylin standing with his back to the door, gazing out the parlour window at the street. The door was open; he had not heard me come in. A glass of brandy was on the table. I had not seen him drink brandy before. Indeed the hotel ought not to have had this contraband drink on the premises. I stood a moment, admiring his tall body and exquisite tailoring. His shoulders drooped, as though he were fatigued, or sad. In the dim light, his caramel hair looked black. The brandy and the weary posture suggested he was disturbed, which told me he had learned of his aunt's infamous carrying-on.

Something stirred in me. I had come with the intention of enjoying his shame, but found that I wanted to comfort him.

'Lord Weylin,' I said softly, to catch his attention.

When he turned, I saw that his expression was troubled. His eyes looked dark, his face drawn. He gazed at me a moment, then a slow smile moved his lips. It crept up to light his eyes in a warm welcome. 'You came alone,' he said. 'I hoped your Mama might have retired.'

'She is still awake, and curious to hear if you learned anything. Bad news, was it?'

He came forward and took my hand to draw me toward the table. We sat. 'No news at all, really.'

I knew he was not telling the truth. His manner, his refusal to look straight at me, were as good as an admission. I put my hand on his wrist and said, 'You can tell me, Weylin. I think I know the secret already. I have been speaking to Steptoe.'

His other hand came out and covered mine in a firm grip. 'I am sorry, Zoie. I had hoped to shield you from the sordid truth. I meant what I said earlier. There is no reason the world need know what your uncle was up to.'

The womanly compassion dwindled to curiosity. 'My uncle? What about your aunt? She is the one who had a lover!'

'Lover?' He looked confused. It darted into my head that he meant to deny it. 'Are you referring to Mr Jones?'

'Of course. And he is young enough to be her son.'

'He *was* her son. That was her guilty secret. I don't know how McShane discovered it, but it is pretty clear he knew, and took advantage of it. There were letters, receipts, a deal of evidence that McShane had been extorting money from my aunt.'

I snatched my hand back. 'I don't believe it! You are making that up to hide her shame.'

'An illegitimate child is hardly less shameful than having a lover,' he said crossly.

I did not really care if Lady Margaret had a whole platoon of illegitimate children. What vexed me was that he had turned Barry back into a scoundrel, just when I thought we had reclaimed him to relative respectability. 'What did you find?'

Weylin put a little heap of papers on the table and began passing them to me, one at a time. The first was a letter from Ireland dated five years before, written during my uncle's short trip home, before coming to live at Hernefield.

I read:

Dear Margaret: While in Dublin I chanced to meet Andrew
Jones. The name, perhaps, will be familiar to you? He is
twenty-five years old. He was teaching in a poor boys'
school here, and living in abominable conditions. I looked
into his history, and know the truth, so do not try to deny it.
He seems a very nice, modest lad. I am shocked that you
should treat him so badly. Remember that, whatever of his
papa, from his mama he carries noble Weylin blood in his
veins.

I am bringing him to England. Something must be done to
better his condition. I shall not embarrass you by making
public what you have done, but I must insist on repairing the
damage to the extent possible. There is no reason your
family need be aware of it. I shall visit my sister, Mrs Barron,
who lives near Parham. You need not publicly recognize him
or me, but we must meet and decide what is to be done about
Andrew. I shall contact you when I arrive. I trust we can
handle this matter amicably. Sincerely, B. J. Barron.

I wanted to take the letter and fling it into the grate, to hide
from the world my uncle's despicable trick. He had ferreted out
Lady Margaret's shameful secret and used it to put her under his
power. Without a word, Weylin handed me another letter. It was
addressed a week later. I read:

I cannot like your suggestion of meeting in London, where
we might be recognized. An out-of-the-way place would
serve our purpose better. I have found a cottage for sale at
Lindfield, ten miles south of Tunbridge Wells. I understand
that you are not wealthy, but MacIntosh cannot have left
you destitute. Have you not got a widow's allowance, or
some jewelry you can sell?

There were other letters. I just glanced at them. They had to do with selling jewelry – a sapphire ring, a ruby brooch – the items Barry sold to Bradford. He wrote, too, of buying the house, and arranging meetings every four months at Lindfield. There was an undertone of menace. Barry did not come right out and say, 'Do it, or I shall trumpet your shame to the world', but the message was there, between the lines. But at least Barry was not after the money for himself; it was for Lady Margaret's illegitimate son.

When I had read the last letter, Weylin gathered them all up and set them aside. 'There is no need to tell your mama about this,' he said. 'McShane and Margaret are dead and gone. I shall track down this Andrew Jones, and see who he is.'

'We know who he is. He is your aunt's by-blow. I see nothing amiss in my uncle helping him.'

'That is what McShane led my aunt to believe,' he replied curtly. 'Obviously Margaret did have a child out of wedlock. I cannot believe she abandoned him to shift for himself in the world. She was not a monster, after all.'

It did seem a little odd that Barry had gone to such pains for a stranger. 'If she knew where he was, then she would not have believed this Andrew Jones was him,' I said uncertainly.

'It is my belief he was sent to India, where such problem lads are often sent. Your uncle ran across him there, or heard the story, and decided to make gain on it. Very likely the lad is dead, and McShane hired a cohort. This plan of extortion would be risky if the real Andrew turned up. I plan to go to London tomorrow and begin investigating there. I shall try to keep your family out of the case when it comes to court. You said your uncle left no sizable estate?'

'Mama had to pay for his burial,' I said.

'Then it seems this Jones fellow got away with the lot. I'll see him behind bars before this is over,' he said angrily.

'That will hardly keep my uncle's name out of it.'

'My hope is that Mr Jones will knuckle under and return what he has stolen without going to court.'

The whole story was so shocking and degrading that it took me a moment to come to terms with it. I unthinkingly poured myself a glass of the brandy and took a healthy swallow. It tasted like fire as it burned its way through me. I immediately fell into a coughing fit, but once that was over, I found the brandy invigorating.

'What makes you so sure Andrew Jones is not your aunt's son? They spent weeks together, over the space of five years. According to Mrs Sangster, your aunt was extremely fond of him. Surely she would recognize her own son.'

'After a quarter of a century? She had not seen him since birth – but that is not to say she simply abandoned him. I cannot and do not believe it. As she never had any other children, she probably wanted to believe he was her son. The pair of them preyed on her guilt and sentiment. It was a despicable thing to do – and it robs her real son of his rightful inheritance, too.'

'I thought he was supposed to be dead, in India.' As I began assessing Weylin's story with a calmer mind, I discovered it was nothing but a tissue of unfounded statements and wild imaginings. 'It seems much more likely to me that Andrew Jones is her son, and my uncle was only trying to shame your aunt into doing as she ought. Surely he had some proof of his identity. A birth document . . . something.'

'What business was it of your uncle's?' he demanded, in no soft voice. 'The fact is, McShane returned from India penniless, and saw his chance to live in luxury off my aunt for the rest of his life.'

'My uncle did not return penniless! He had five thousand pounds, which vanished. And he lived on his pension. He did not live at Lindfield. Only your aunt and her son met there.'

'And my aunt's male servant. The description I had from Mrs

Sangster sounds like McShane. I mean to take one of those sketches of McShane to show her. I daresay we shall discover the servant was no one else but your uncle.'

'You will not take one of my sketches, sir. My uncle was not sunk to waiting on your aunt and her bastard, I assure you. As to his living in luxury at your aunt's expense, I would hardly call that little cottage the lap of luxury. You are quick to jump to conclusions that suit you, milord! Your only concern is that Jones diddled you out of your aunt's money.'

'There is more than money at issue here. Two unscrupulous men were preying on a vulnerable old lady, feeding her lies, terrorizing her. They are worse than thieves.'

'I will not sit here and listen to my uncle being traduced in this manner when he cannot defend himself. Talk about unscrupulous men preying on a vulnerable lady! You have no proof for any of this.'

'I soon will have. I shall leave for London early tomorrow to find Mr Jones and beat the truth out of the scoundrel.'

'You had best be very sure of your facts, sir, for if you slander my uncle, you will hear from my solicitor.'

I flounced out of the parlour in high dudgeon. No words followed me about sparing my family shame. So much for his fine claim! I ran upstairs to tell Mama what had happened. Her agitation was as great as my own. We enjoyed a quarter of an hour's heated tirade against Lord Weylin, then decided to send for a pot of tea, as it was clear we would not be getting any sleep that night.

By the second cup, we had calmed down sufficiently to speak sensibly. 'If it were true,' Mama said, fingering her chin to aid concentration, 'how did Barry come to discover Mr Jones was Lady Margaret's by-blow, as it seems Mr Jones did not know himself? How did Barry suspect she ever had this illegitimate child? Do you think someone in Ireland was the father?'

Then the truth struck me with the force of a blow. 'Good God! Could Andrew be Barry's son?'

'Barry was the best-looking of all his set, no denying.'

'Why the devil did he not marry her?'

'Perhaps he did not know of her condition. Lady Margaret was still in Ireland when he went to India. I wonder how he learned of it. I daresay she wrote and told him, but it takes such an age for a letter to reach India, and then for him to have to sail back home . . . It would be too late. The child would already be born. I really think that is what happened, Zoie. Why else would Barry be at such pains to see the lad was taken care of? And it would explain what happened to his own money as well. He gave it to Andrew, as he should.'

I could not like this version of the story either. It put Barry in a bad light, ruining a young lady, then merrily running away and leaving her to her fate. As I thought over the tone of his letters to Lady Margaret, I thought he took pretty high ground, blaming her for abandoning their son when he had abandoned both of them. He should have been begging her forgiveness. But that is the way. Two people misbehave, and it is the lady – and the child – who bear the brunt of it.

'We shan't tell Lord Weylin what we think,' Mama said. 'It is all done and over with now. No point slandering the dead.'

'What of the living, Mama? Weylin plans to get the money back from Andrew Jones. He thinks Jones is an impostor. I fear we must tell him the truth.'

'Plague of a man. Why can he not leave well enough alone? They cannot put us in jail, can they, Zoie? We have done nothing wrong – but it would be wrong to say nothing when we know the truth.'

'We do not actually know it,' I said uncertainly.

'In my bones, I know it,' Mama said wearily. 'I always

wondered that Barry showed no interest whatsoever in Lady Margaret when he came to stay with us. She was still a handsome lady, but he never looked within a right angle of her. He did not want me to notice anything between them, you see. What he should have done was to marry her – belatedly, to be sure, but better late than never. A scoundrel to the end, and he was such a nice, jolly boy.'

'You must tell Weylin, Mama. He plans to go to London early tomorrow and begin making trouble for Mr Jones.'

'I shall mention it, but of course, we have no proof. Very likely he will try to get Barry's five thousand into the bargain. That belongs to my nephew.'

That 'nephew' came out as if Mama had been saying it forever. How quickly she had accepted the idea. If her suspicions were true – and she knew Barry better than anyone else did – then I had a new cousin. I was curious to see what Cousin Andrew was like. I was also apprehensive to consider meeting Lord Weylin with this new version of the story, which threw an even more degrading light on Barry.

In the confusion of our discussion, I had overlooked the fact that Mrs Sangster, at the post office, had not recognized Barry. If he had been staying at Lindfield with Lady Margaret, she must have seen him. Perhaps he had stayed close to the house. Then, too, I had shown her an altered sketch, and said he was a clergyman. She would hardly think of connecting a servant with a clergyman. Would she recognize him without his clerical collar and the moustache? That could easily enough be checked.

Cousin Andrew – he was Weylin's cousin, too. Odd that we were now connections, just when he must be wishing he had never heard of us.

Chapter Fifteen

$\mathcal{A}$s I lay in bed staring at the invisible ceiling, I reflected on the curious situation we had uncovered.

I liked to think that Andrew, Lady Margaret, and Barry had enjoyed some happy days at Lindfield. I understood now why they had all stuck close to the house. They just wanted to be together, away from the prying eyes of the world. Lady Margaret doted on the boy, the locals said. That suggested that she, at least, had enjoyed having her son back. I could not like that my uncle was sunk to posing as their servant. As Lady Margaret had become Mrs Langtree, why could he not have been Mr Langtree, and Andrew their son? Did Andrew know he was their son, or did they tell him he was "Mrs Langtree's" nephew?

Both Mama and I looked like hags when we went down to the private parlour in the morning. A sleepless night is enough to destroy a lady's face, and when shame and worry are added on top, it is hard to keep up any countenance at all. I was not too unhappy to find the parlour unoccupied.

When we entered, the waiter said, 'His lordship had breakfast early and has left for London. He said to inform you that he would be gone for a few days, madam.'

My first reaction was relief. The inevitable had been staved off temporarily. Then I thought of Cousin Andrew, and knew we could not let Weylin go about his business unchecked.

As soon as we had ordered breakfast and got rid of the waiter, I said, 'We must stop Weylin, Mama.'

'I shall write and tell him what I believe to be the truth, Zoie, for I cannot face a trip to London at this time.'

'Would you not like to see Cousin Andrew?' I asked.

'I would, but I am less eager to see Lord Weylin. Best to tell him the truth in a letter, and let him digest it before we have to see him again.'

The letter was much discussed over breakfast. After our plates were cleared away, we asked for pen and paper, and Mama wrote her explanation in a simple, straightforward way. She expressed regret, and the hope that Lord Weylin would not treat Mr Jones harshly. Whatever of the others, he, at least, was an innocent victim. When we were satisfied with the letter, she gave it to the waiter for posting to Weylin's London residence.

'Can we go home now?' Mama asked weakly.

I would have liked to take an unaltered sketch of Barry to Mrs Sangster for confirmation that he was Mrs Langtree's servant, but Mama looked so worn, I could not ask her to stay longer. We called our carriage. You may imagine my chagrin when I saw that wretch of a Steptoe sitting saucily on the box beside Rafferty. Steptoe lifted his hat and said, 'Good morning, ladies.'

When Rafferty let down the stairs, he said to Mama, 'He asked if he could hitch a lift. I hope you don't mind, ma'am?'

'It is no matter,' Mama said. She was beyond caring.

We did not talk much on the way home. I noticed Mama's frown dwindle to a bemused smile about halfway along the road, and knew she was thinking of Cousin Andrew. I thought of him, too, wondering what he was like, and whether the Weylins would acknowledge him. Of course, Mama would. Irish families are close, and if the Duke of Clarence can vaunt his dozen or so by-blows, why should we hang our heads in shame at claiming one?

'We shall invite my nephew to Hernefield for a visit after this is all cleared away, Zoie,' Mama said as the carriage arrived home. 'A pity you were in such a rush to dismantle the octagonal tower. He might have liked to use his papa's room.'

I had lost my enthusiasm for art lessons since learning Count Borsini was a fraud. I would dismiss him, and continue with my work unaided, but as the tower was already dismantled, I would use it as my studio. It was good to be home, even if the future was uncertain. I was even happy to have Brodagan jawing at us again.

'I see Steptoe is back like a bad penny,' she said. 'I hoped we'd seen the back of him.' She said a deal more; there was no fault in the world but Steptoe had it. 'Where has he been? That is what I would like to know, and I will. The gander's beak is no longer than the goose's when it comes to rooting out the truth. If it was a wrong he was doing you, melady, it'll come back on him in time.'

There would be a breaking and bruising of bones belowstairs, but I had other things to worry about. I went straight up to the attic and searched through every box and bag Barry had brought home with him, hoping to find some confirmation or contradiction of Mama's suspicions. Lady Margaret must have answered those letters he had written to her. She may even have written to him when he was in India. That was my major activity for the next two days. After going through everything twice, I was convinced Barry had not kept the letters, or anything else of an incriminating nature.

His death had not been sudden. He had faded away slowly over a period of two weeks – ample time to be rid of the evidence of his past sins. Barry had, presumably, told Andrew of his mother's passing. I wondered how the poor fellow had heard of his father's death. It seemed wrong that the newly found son had not attended the funeral of either parent. As I thought of these things, Andrew began to seem like a real person to me, with worries and troubles of his own.

Who had raised him? Was he what we call a gentleman? He had been teaching in a boys' school, so at least he had been educated. It was difficult to form any idea of his appearance. Lady Margaret was blonde and soft-featured and plump. Barry was tall and dark and lean. Whatever the physical attractions of his youth, by the time I met Barry, he had hardened to a somewhat bitter man, with his skin tanned by the tropical sun of India.

Yet there had been occasional flashes of a warmer personality lurking below the surface. Sometimes when we had company, Barry would expand a little on his experiences in India, especially if the company included ladies. And when he chaperoned my lessons with Count Borsini, he and the count often fell into lively conversation, as two well-traveled gentlemen will do. Barry used to speak of his Indian adventures, and Borsini told tales of his life in Italy.

It would soon be time for another lesson with Borsini. To avoid it, I wrote to Aldershot and told him I no longer felt the need of his tutelage. I thanked him very civilly for past help, but made quite clear the lessons were over.

Steptoe continued on with us, without any change in salary. He was a reformed character, and we were too distracted to want the bother of finding a replacement. By Sunday, Weylin had still not returned from London. The length of his visit caused considerable worry at Hernefield. He had not deigned to reply to mama's letter, so we had no idea what course he was following. It did not even occur to us to apply to Parham for information. We had no idea whether he had informed his mama what was afoot.

On Monday the painters came to paint my studio. I went upstairs with them to give instructions. Brodagan could not miss the opportunity to order two grown men about, and went with us. She cast one look at the floor and said, 'I told Steptoe to see this matting was rolled up and put away. They'll destroy it with paint drops.'

'It hardly matters, Brodagan. It is already a shambles.'

'A shambles, is it? It is a deal better than the wee scrap of rug in my room.'

'We'll not harm it, missus,' the painter in charge assured her, 'for we'll lay this here tarpaulin over it.' As he spoke, he took one end of the tarpaulin, his helper the other, and they placed it carefully over the shabby old matting.

They opened the container of paint and began stirring it up. It looked a very stark white. I left them to it, and went belowstairs just as Mama was putting on her bonnet.

'I am driving into Aldershot, Zoie,' she said. 'I want to get new muslin for Andrew's sheets. And perhaps new draperies for the blue guest room. They have got so very faded.'

'We are not sure he will come, Mama, but the new sheets and even draperies will not go amiss. I shall stay home to keep an eye on my studio. This paint looks very cold. I may change the shade after they have done half a wall.'

'I shan't be long.'

She left, and I took my pad to the garden to try my hand at sketching the gardener, who was working with the roses in front of the house. As there was no convenient seat, I sat on the grass and studied the gardener a moment, choosing the most artful pose for my sketch. It would be a full-length action drawing. He changed position so often that it was difficult to draw him. As he only gave us two afternoons a week, I did not like to disrupt his work and ask him to stand still.

Borsini had been teaching me a new exercise for drawing people in motion. It involved moving the pencil in quick circles to suggest movement. He was quite a dab at it, but when I had tried, I ended up with a whirl that looked like the onset of a tornado. I tried this technique again, and began dashing off an arm composed of circles. The gardener moved; I sketched more quickly. The more quickly I sketched, the larger the arm grew, until in the end I had executed yet another tornado, whirling off the edge of the page.

I was interrupted by the sound of an approaching carriage. I thought it was Weylin, and my heart raced, but when I looked to the road, I saw it was a jaunty little gig, drawn by a single nag. Mrs Chawton drives such a rig, but hers is black. This one was a more dashing affair altogether, in dark green, with a handsome bay pulling it. As it came closer, I saw the man holding the reins was a gentleman, to judge by his curled beaver and blue jacket. Cousin Andrew!

I hurried forward, and saw that it was Count Borsini. He usually rode a hack, or in bad weather, we sent the carriage for him. My annoyance with him gushed forth. If he had come to try to talk me into continuing the lessons, I would let him know his game was up. He drew to a stop and lifted his hat.

'*Buongiorno, Signorina* Barron. How do you like this, eh?' he asked smiling in his old conning way. 'What a pleasure to have the reins of a carriage between my fingers again. I have missed it. At the Villa Borsini I used to drive Papa's team.'

I had always found him attractive. Really quite handsome, and his charm and his few foreign phrases made him appear dashing.

He has chestnut hair and blue eyes. His features are regular, his physique adequate, though on the slender side.

'You must be doing well for yourself, Borsini,' I said, running an eye over the rig. 'Very handsome.'

'Papa's wine did well last year. We even sold some to the Vatican – a great honor. Papa sent me a little bonus. I have come to see if you would like a ride in my chariot.'

Occasionally I had an outing with Borsini, besides my lessons. These outings were chaperoned by my uncle, and usually involved art in one way or another. We had been to a few exhibitions, and he took me to other artists' studios a few times. Once he went shopping for art supplies with me, as he did not approve of the brushes I used. We had never before gone out driving unchaperoned, just for pleasure. Of course, he had not had a rig before, so he could hardly ask me.

'Actually, I am busy,' I said.

He looked across the grass, spotted my sketchpad, and picked it up. 'Good! I am happy to see it is only Borsini you are abandoning, and not your art.' That was his only verbal reproof, but his soulful eyes made me feel like a murderer. He glanced at the tornado and shook his head. 'You have not got the knack of this technique. It is like this. *Prego*?' He took the pencil from my hand, whirled it about for a moment, and with absolute sleight of hand had soon done a good likeness of the gardener. I could almost see the man's movements in those whirling circles.

Whatever Weylin might say, Borsini was a good artist. What if the prince had not commissioned him to do his painting? What if he did need the money? Was that not a reason to continue the lessons, rather than cancel them? Perhaps Cousin Andrew's position influenced my thinking. I often thought of him, a poor fellow, cast off to shift for himself, until he was rescued.

Borsini handed the sketchpad back, smiling at me. 'I think you could still use a few lessons, *signorina*,' he said. 'If it is the money – psh!' he tossed up his hands in disdain. 'As I said, I have come into a few hundred pounds. I would be happy to go on teaching you without payment. It is a shame to stop, just when you are making such strides.'

'I shall have to think about it, Borsini.'

'I hope I have not done something to offend you?'

'No, of course not.'

'*Grazie*,' he said, with an elaborate bow that would look absurd if performed by an Englishman. It involved clutching the heart, as if to quell its rampage.

'How is our – *your* studio coming along?' he asked, in a wistful sort of way. It was Borsini who first suggested I ought to have a studio. I think he had been looking forward to it quite as much as I.

'The painters are at work on it this minute. I meant to check. The white they are using on the walls looks very stark.'

'You don't want a dead white. A little yellow, or red *addolci* – how would you say – softens the effect.'

'Will you come and have a look with me?'

'*Delizioso!* I shall just run my gig around to the stable.'

I asked the gardener to take care of the gig, and we went into the house together. Steptoe was not at the door to admit us. He was gradually returning to his uppity ways, but his days were numbered. Brodagan had been peeking out the window at Borsini, with whom she had fallen in love, and came to meet us. He flirts with her, and even tackles a brogue, to please her.

'Brodagan, me old flower,' he said, handing her his hat. 'Have you missed me?'

'When did I ever have time to miss anyone?' she asked, in her grim way. 'Between answering the door and cooking and cleaning and fixing up melady's studio, I wouldn't have time to miss my own self.'

'Ah, but we would all miss you if you left us, me darlin',' he said with a laugh.

'I'll fetch you a cup of tea,' Brodagan said. She simpered, curtsied, and went happily on her way, carrying his hat as if it were a priceless crown.

Borsini looked after her retreating form. 'Whatever of our lessons, *signorina*, you must let me paint Brodagan. It would be a crime for posterity not to have a picture of that steeple she has constructed atop her head. I adore her.'

'And she dotes on you, Borsini.'

'She will bring us tea strong enough for a mouse to trot across. That is the way they take it in Ireland, no?'

'And at Hernefield. The studio is on the third floor. It is a bit of a climb,' I said, leading him up the stairs.

Borsini looked all about him as we reached the landing. It was the first time he had got abovestairs, but I think he might have quelled his curiosity. When he saw my displeasure, he said, 'I was just wondering which is your room, Miss Barron.' '*Signorina*' usually settles down to 'Miss Barron' after a few minutes conversation.

'You cannot see it from here,' I said, continuing toward the narrower staircase leading to the octagonal tower. The smell of paint came down the staircase to greet us. At the top, a blinding wall of white stared at us like a snowbank.

Borsini made a strangled sound in his throat and hid his eyes. 'The glare! The glare! It is blinding! *Fermata!* Stop this vandalism at once!'

The painters looked at him as if he were mad. He darted forward and snatched the paintbrushes from their hands. 'It will be winter in your studio twelve months of the year if you continue with this crime against the human spirit. Yellow. Bring me a golden yellow pigment, bright as the sun, and I, Borsini, shall create a color to bring warmth to this studio.'

Already the studio seemed warmer. I decided I would continue my lessons for the time being.

Chapter Sixteen

orsini personally oversaw the blending of the oil paints. The workers had brought colored paints with them for mixing. Borsini had cans of red and yellow, gold as the summer sun, opened, and mixed a portion of both in with the white to achieve the proper shade. Of course, he removed his jacket to avoid getting paint on it. Before long, Mary, the maid, came to tell us tea was ready, but as Borsini was in the throes of creation, he ignored her.

'We shall be down in a moment, Mary,' I said. 'Or would you like your tea now, Borsini?'

'Later, *per cortesìa.*'

Mary left, and Borsini continued mixing and stirring. He added another two or three drops of red to the white paint, stirred it up, and applied a daub to the wall. '*Ecco!* That is the shade I wanted. The first pale saffron blush of sunrise over the Grand Canal.'

It was a pretty shade, nearly white, but with a flush of color to remove the harshness. I approved, and suggested we go down to tea.

'Presently,' he said. 'I want to remain just a moment longer, picturing to myself *Signorina* Barron at her easel.' His moist eyes toured the room. I thought his lower lip trembled, but I could not be sure.

'Picture Count Borsini with her,' I said. 'You are right. I do require more lessons.'

His whole face glowed. 'Ah, *signorina!* You are too kind!' In his excitement, he grasped my hands, and would have kissed me if the painters had not been squinting at him.

I was trying to disentangle my hands from his when Brodagan's sharp voice brought me to attention. 'Checking on the painters, is it? It's a good thing I came up, for you need someone to check on you, my girl.'

Brodagan's tone told me she was not happy to see me stealing her beau. I turned to her, and saw, to my horror, that she had brought Lord Weylin up with her. 'His lordship wants a word with you,' she said. 'If you don't get downstairs, the tea will be cold as ice.'

'Miss Barron,' Weylin said, with a curt, graceless bow. His eyes moved to Borsini, taking in his paint-smeared hands, his jacket-less body, his smiling face, and condemning the whole without uttering a word.

'Allow me to present Count Borsini, my art teacher,' I said. 'Count Borsini, this is my neighbor, Lord Weylin.'

Borsini performed a flourishing bow, then stuck out his hand, as Weylin had extended his. '*Scusi,*' Borsini said, noticing the paint on his fingers. My own were daubed as well.

'We need turpentine,' I said, and escaped to fetch it and a clean rag, while Brodagan helped Borsini on with his jacket.

'Doing a little redecorating, Miss Barron?' Weylin asked, while we wiped away the paint.

'This will be my studio,' I explained. 'Count Borsini was kind enough to help me choose the color.'

'One would obviously require assistance for such a demanding task,' he said, with a satirical glint in his eyes.

'Yes, I am happy I consulted him, for the painters were using a horrid, cold white. It takes the artist's touch.'

We all went belowstairs for tea. I was happy to see Borsini controlled his passion for Latin tricks. He did not sprinkle his conversation with Italian phrases, or call Weylin *signor*, or whatever the Italian word for milord might be. I had noticed before that these Latin airs were confined to ladies. When he conversed with Barry, for instance, he spoke only English, with a light accent.

Of course, I was on nettles to hear what Weylin had to say about London and Mr Jones, but that conversation must wait until Borsini had left. He stuck like a barnacle. I think he sensed a potential client in Weylin, and was at pains to charm him. He spoke of the medieval architecture of Parham, and inquired minutely into its history. Strangely, Weylin seemed equally interested in the artist, while paying only a polite minimum of attention to myself.

'As you are an artist, you might be interested in the Van Dycks at Parham, Count,' he said. 'Van Dyck painted a few of my ancestors in the last century.'

Borsini opened his mouth to correct that erroneous date. Of course, he knew perfectly well Van Dyck had painted in the seventeenth century, but he was too polite to reveal Weylin as an ignoramus. 'That would be charming, milord. Do you have any Italian paintings? They, of course, are of interest to me. My papa has some wonderful Titians. The loggia at Villa Borsini has a mural ascribed to Raphael.'

Weylin smiled like a cat. He thought he was proving Borsini a fake. 'I believe I can show you a few Renaissance pictures worth the trip,' he said. 'Your papa's villa, Count – just where is it, exactly?'

'In Tuscany,' Borsini said. 'We have vast vineyards in Tuscany.' He did not say a word about the palazzo in Venice.

I was sure that villa in Tuscany had begun life as a palazzo in Venice. I had mentioned at the time my surprise to hear there were vineyards in that watery spot.

'I do not recall ever seeing a Borsini wine,' Weylin said, looking innocent.

'The English prefer claret, or sherry.' Borsini smiled forgivingly. 'My papa sent me several cases of his excellent Chianti, if you are interested to try it, Lord Weylin.'

'I should like that very much. Is your schedule quite full at the moment, Count, or would it be possible for you to execute a small commission for me?'

Borsini smiled in delight. 'I can always make time for such patrons as yourself, milord. Is it a portrait of yourself, or some member of your family, you wish for?'

'Actually, it is my mama's pug dog,' Weylin said. 'Mama's birthday is not far off, and I require a present for her.'

'Count Borsini does not paint dogs!' I said angrily.

Borsini just gave a tight little smile. 'Lord Weylin wishes to see an example of my skill, before committing himself to a portrait. Am I right, milord?' Weylin did not deny it. 'It is not necessary to waste time painting a dog. Come to my studio in Aldershot.'

'Why did you set up shop in Aldershot, when your noble connections would assure you plentiful patrons in London?' Weylin asked. His suspicious tone cast aspersions on Borsini's claim to a title.

'My preferred customers nowadays are trees, milord, which are plentiful in this delightful neighborhood.'

'Surely trees do not commission portraits?'

'When I need money, I shake the family trees,' Borsini said, smiling tenaciously throughout this rude catechism. 'I have no trouble finding customers for my landscapes as well.'

'I shall call at your studio tomorrow,' Weylin said.

'That will be satisfactory. I am at liberty between two and five.'

'Let us say four-thirty,' Weylin said.

I looked to Borsini, hoping he had got what he wanted, and would now leave us. I was out-of-reason cross when it was Weylin who rose and said he must be leaving.

'Oh, do stay, Weylin!' I said. 'Have another cup of tea.'

'Another time, Miss Barron.' Then he turned to Borsini. 'Are you free now, Count? Are you quite happy with the color of Miss Barron's studio? Perhaps you would like to see the Van Dycks – and the Titians – while you are in the neighborhood. I shall tell my groom to take you back to Aldershot. No need for Miss Barron to have her team harnessed up.'

'Borsini has his own carriage,' I said.

Borsini looked surprised at Weylin's eagerness, but he did not object. 'We have not settled when I shall come for your lesson, Miss Barron,' he said. 'Shall we say the day after tomorrow, if the weather is fine? You will want to give your studio time to dry, and be aired out before using it.'

'You may come tomorrow. I should prefer to paint outdoors, if the weather is good.' The studio required a chaperon. I had not yet confirmed when Mrs Chawton wished to begin her lessons, and in any case, I wanted to get Borsini alone to discover what happened at Parham, and at his studio with Weylin. I felt in my bones that Weylin was only making sport of the man. I had not expected this petty streak in him.

I sent off for the gentlemen's carriages, with a little twinge of embarrassment that Borsini's vehicle was so humble. It looked like a toy beside Weylin's crested traveling coach and team of four. When I saw what Weylin was driving, I realized he had not been to Parham yet. He had stopped here even before going home. That suggested some urgency, yet he was leaving without saying a word about Mr Jones.

Brodagan was once more on duty at the door. While she carried on her *à suivie* flirtation with Borsini, Weylin said, 'Where is Steptoe? Have you dismissed him?'

'No, I waited to hear from you first. We must talk. When can you come back?'

'I am flattered at your eagerness, Zoie,' he said, chewing back a mischievous grin.

'You are delighted at thinking you have proved Borsini a fraud, is what you mean. He knows very well when Van Dyck was painting. He just did not wish to embarrass you.'

'Well now, that is the mark of a real gentleman. But I shall taste his papa's wine, and read the label on the bottle, before I am satisfied.'

'I cannot imagine what you have against the poor man. What harm has he ever done you?'

'That is what I am trying to discover, Zoie. But if he is a count, I'll eat my hat.'

Borsini escaped from Brodagan and joined us. 'I really must paint that woman!' he said, flushed with success. 'It would take El Greco to do her justice. There is such delightful malice in her visage. An original.'

'I think you would enjoy to paint Lady Weylin, too,' I said.

Weylin shot a questioning look at me. He was uncertain whether that was a slur on his mama, or an effort to land the commission for Borsini. 'That will be up to Mama,' he said, and headed out the door with Borsini.

I was obliged to call out after him, which annoyed me. 'You have not said when you will come back, Weylin.'

'The road goes both ways, Zoie. If you are eager for my company, you know where I live. Mama don't bite, you know, even if she does occasionally bark.'

I slammed the door and uttered a few words not learned in the schoolroom. Brodagan sailed out from the saloon, where she had been stacking the tea tray. 'It is good to see Count Borsini making a few decent friends,' she said, with something strangely like a smile. 'Lord Weylin would recognize quality when he was hit in the face with it.'

'Yes, I am afraid he would,' I said, and went back up to look at the studio.

It was pretty clear that Weylin planned to expose Borsini as a fraud. Whatever clients the count had managed to round up would leave him. He would be forced to remove from Aldershot to Bath or some town farther away, where no one had heard of him. I was certain the Palazzo Borsini had always been at Venice. Yet if he actually had wine from the Borsini vineyard . . . As I pondered this, it occurred to me that Borsini had got hold of wine with such a label, and transferred his imaginary palazzo to a villa in Tuscany. That would account for it.

It was a foolish thing to do, but an artist led a precarious existence. Adding a title to his name would bring in a few clients, and he was not doing anyone any harm. So why had Weylin decided to ruin him? Was it possible he was jealous? That, while flattering, did not ring true. Weylin's real interest during the visit had been on Borsini, not me.

When I went downstairs, Mama had returned from her shopping trip. I told her of Weylin's visit. Her face blanched. 'What happened in London?' she demanded.

'He could not tell me in front of Borsini. They left together. I expect Weylin will return, sooner or later.'

'Surely he will come back this evening. Was he angry?'

'No. He behaved more . . . mischievously,' I said. 'I cannot make heads or tails of it, Mama, but he did not seem angry.'

'Then he has managed to get poor Andrew's money away from him; depend upon it.'

This seemed entirely likely, and I was surprised I had not thought of it myself. It was yet another offence in Weylin's dish. Whenever he deigned to return, he would hear a few things to turn his ears red.

Mama showed me the new drapery material, a pretty royal blue sateen, that would enliven the blue guest room. We tried to cheer ourselves by imagining Andrew's future visit, but our hearts were not in it.

Chapter Seventeen

Lord Weylin did not call that evening. I had a note from Mrs Chawton informing me that the first meeting of the Book Society would take place at her house at eight. I had been looking forward to it with keen pleasure, but wrote putting it off in expectation of seeing Weylin. When I went in search of a servant to deliver my message, Steptoe made a hissing sound from the hallway, and beckoned me to him.

'I am not a snake, Steptoe. If you wish to speak to me, pray use the King's English. What do you want?' I demanded.

He handed me a note. 'From his lordship,' he said with a leer. 'His footman left this billy doo, with instructions to give it to you on the sly, miss.' He put his finger to his lips and said, 'Mum's the word.'

'This is not a billet-doux, but an ordinary note,' I said, and snatched it from his fingers. My heart was racing, but whether it was from annoyance with Steptoe or anticipation of my billet-doux, I could not determine.

'I wager it's an invitation to tea, miss.' Steptoe smirked. 'I wonder why his lordship wanted secrecy.'

The note was sealed with wax. I examined it to see Steptoe had not read it before me. The seal did not appear to have been tampered with. I gave him the note for Mrs Chawton and told Mama I was going up to my studio, as I wanted privacy to read my note. *Was* it a billet-doux? That would explain Weylin's efforts to discredit Borsini, if he feared I was romantically interested in the count; I did not go to the studio, but to my bedroom. My fingers were trembling as I broke the wax seal. The letter was long enough to require two sheets of paper.

I read:

Zoie. I am sending this to you privately. It is for you to decide how much to tell your mama. I did not find Andrew Jones in London, but I spoke to his lawyer. There is documented evidence that Jones is the illegitimate son of my aunt – and your uncle. My aunt did not make any other Will than the one read at Parham. She arranged to hand over her worldly goods to her son before dying. Naturally I shall not interfere in the arrangement. It seems reasonable to assume that your uncle's missing money was also given to Jones.

I have heard from Mrs Riddle, Lady Margaret's companion. She confirmed that my aunt gave birth to a male child six months after her marriage, and the family set about the story that it was a legitimate miscarriage. Apparently Mr MacIntosh was aware of Margaret's condition when he married her. He made the stipulation that the child be put out for adoption, and arranged the matter himself. My aunt was not told where the baby went, and promised not to try to find him. One can feel some sympathy with her. She must have been at her wits' end when McShane shabbed off, leaving her with child. I can forgive her; whether you can forgive your uncle is another matter. I own I find it difficult.

That is no reason to punish Mr Jones, however. I am making queries to find him, to see if he needs any further assistance. As we agreed at Tunbridge, this matter will be kept *entre nous*. If you have any questions, you can find me here. I shall be at Parham for the next while. Please let me know whether you are telling your mama or not, so that I shall know what to say – and what not to say – when I meet her.

On a happier note, Mama likes your Count Borsini amazingly. She (and Bubbums) are to sit for him. He has agreed to begin her portrait tomorrow afternoon, canceling all lessons for the present, and has asked that I make his apologies to you. He will not be able to keep his appointment. I felt sure you would not object, as this will do his career good. We might get the prince to sit for him yet!

I hope the news regarding your uncle does not distress you overly much. There may have been extenuating circumstances. I have not told Mama any of this yet, so if you are speaking to her, please bear it in mind.

Your servant, Weylin.

I read the note twice, then read it again to see if there was anything that should be kept from Mama. As she already knew, or believed, that Barry was deeply involved, there seemed no harm in showing her the letter. Despite Steptoe's leers and smirks, there was no air of romance about it. Weylin did not even say he would call. I would find him (by which he meant a note) at Parham if I had any questions. That indicated that, while he was willing to forgive my uncle, he had no wish to strengthen the acquaintance with the family.

It seemed hard that he should steal Borsini away as well. I disliked, too, the offhand way he did it, without even consulting me first. Of course, a portrait of the countess might indeed do Borsini's reputation a world of good, so I tried to be happy for him. I took the letter down to Mama. When she had digested it, we had a long talk. It was not Borsini or Weylin's high handedness that interested her.

'So Weylin has found out the truth,' she said, with a little sigh of relief. 'He is not so out-of-reason cross as I feared. When he finds my nephew, we shall invite Andrew here for a visit. What would do the lad more good is if Weylin would take an interest in him. He could make him an MP, or get him a position with the government. You must talk Weylin into it.'

'I doubt Weylin will put himself out for an illegitimate cousin,' I said.

'At least he does not plan to hound Andrew for the money. I believe Weylin is right in thinking there were extenuating circumstances. Perhaps Barry did not know Lady Margaret was enceinte when he went to India. He was never that bad.'

'He certainly knew they were not married when he seduced her, Mama! That is bad enough.'

'So he did, but so did she know it. It is for the lady to maintain proper conduct. This is not all Barry's fault.'

Brodagan brought the tea tray, and by the time we had taken tea, Mama was waxing quite cheerful. She spoke as though it were all settled that Andrew would be a part of both families, yet we hadn't the least notion what sort of a man he was. I hoped she would not be too disappointed.

The evening seemed endless. Until the clock chimed ten times, I was on pins and needles, listening for the sound of a carriage approaching, or a knock at the door. At ten I knew it was too late to hear from Weylin, and went up to bed.

The morning brought new hope. It was a fine, sunny day. Soft balls of cloud looked like whipped cream against the blue sky. I made a careful toilette, and sat in ladylike idleness all the morning long in the saloon, listening once more for the sound of the door knocker. Mama busied herself preparing the guest room for her nephew, whom she was rapidly turning into the son she never had.

Over lunch the talk was all of Andrew. Would my mount suit him, she wondered, or should she look about for a larger one? A gentleman would require a mount. But perhaps he already had one. She would wait until he came, and if he wanted one, he could choose it himself. She would have him ride over that west pasture, and see if it needed tilling. Papa used to speak of it. Perhaps Andrew would want the double-pedestal desk from the study in his bedroom. The desk presently there was only a token. She would have Brodagan arrange it that very day.

'For goodness' sake, Mama, it is not even certain he is coming. Before you give him Papa's desk and my mount, let us see if he wants to visit us – and whether he is the sort of man we want in the house. God only knows how he was raised. He may be a Captain Sharp or a heathen, for all we know.'

'I am sure he was raised a gentleman,' Mama said.

'What makes you so sure? It was MacIntosh who arranged his adoption. He would hardly look fondly on his wife's by-blow.'

'He was teaching at a school, Zoie, so he must be educated.'

'He was not teaching at Eton or Harrow. It was a poor boys' school, probably for orphans. He was living in one room. Barry was astonished at his low circumstances.'

'Yes, dear, but Andrew would have smartened himself up by now. Barry gave him all that money.'

'Yes, and so did Lady Margaret. Whatever else he is, he certainly knows how to look out for his own interests.'

'Zoie, that is uncharitable! Remember, he is your cousin.'

'And you remember he is only your nephew, Mama. Next you will be saying you ought to leave him Hernefield.'

147

'Oh, not the whole thing, Zoie,' she laughed. 'Only a stipulation that he can always be assured of a home here.'

'Let us wait until we have met him, before taking him on as a tenant for life,' I said. I was beginning to hope Weylin did not succeed in finding the elusive Andrew Jones.

One can sit still, waiting, for only so long. The walls of Hernefield were beginning to weigh down on me. As Borsini was painting Lady Weylin, Lord Weylin was quite at liberty, but he did not bother to drive the few miles to Hernefield. He was out in his reckoning if he thought I was going to sit home all day long waiting for him. After lunch, I drove into Aldershot to call on Mrs Chawton. She was not at home. I stopped at the art supply shop while I was there, to purchase some pigments and my extra easel. Rafferty let me down at the shop.

It was a busy place, since all the ladies had taken up watercolors. The oil pigments, less in demand, were kept in a special nook at the rear of the shop. I slid past the watercolor ladies, speaking to a few of them whom I recognized, and continued toward the nook. As I approached it, I spotted Borsini, bent over the shelves, selecting paints.

'Borsini, what are you doing here?' I exclaimed.

'*Signorina* Barron! What a delightful surprise. I have come to buy supplies for my portrait of Lady Weylin. You have heard of my commission?'

'Indeed I have. Congratulations.'

'I am sorry to have to postpone your lesson.'

As he was not painting this afternoon, I wondered why he had not slipped my lesson in. 'Lady Weylin will not want to sit both morning and afternoon,' I said.

'She prefers mornings, when she is rested.'

'Then you can come to me one afternoon.'

Lord Weylin appeared from behind the rack of pigments. 'Miss

Barron! I thought I recognized your voice.' He bowed.

I curtsied. As I was "Miss Barron" Weylin became "Lord Weylin". 'Lord Weylin. I did not realize you were interested in painting.'

'Mostly in Mama's portrait,' he replied. 'Borsini has kindly agreed to stay with us for the two weeks of the sitting. I drove him to town as he will require a larger carriage to transport his clothing and supplies.'

Borsini moving into Parham for two weeks? This was conde-scension of a high order. Even stranger was that Weylin should turn his carriage into a tranter's wagon, and become Borsini's servant.

Bereft of a sensible reply, I said, 'I see.'

'I have been to Borsini's studio,' Weylin continued. 'He showed me some of your work. Very nice.' The only work of mine Borsini had was a couple of sketches of myself.

Borsini said, 'Lord Weylin particularly liked a seascape I painted at Brighton. You know the one, Miss Barron, with the bathing houses.'

Borsini had painted several scenes of Brighton, which he sold to tourists as a souvenir of their visit to the seaside. He dashed these potboilers off quickly to make money. They were pretty, but not what a connoisseur would purchase.

I exchanged a secret smile with Borsini. 'Oh yes, I recall the seascapes. Lord Weylin has chosen well.'

Borsini feared I would say more, and rushed in to ask how my studio was coming along.

'The color you chose is excellent. The painters are just finish-ing up. I have come to buy oils and another easel. Like you, I shall have more than one work going at a time.'

'I want to show you some new brushes they have just got in,' Borsini said. 'Fine badger-hair brushes. I cannot like those cheap pig-bristle ones you still use from time to time, Miss Barron. They leave their mark in the pigment. They are too hard.'

Weylin followed along as we examined the brushes. When Borsini had talked me into three of the expensive sort, the talk turned to easels. Weylin's nose was out of joint at being ignored.

When my selections were made, he said, 'You had best pick out your pigments, Borsini. I shall bear Miss Barron company while her purchases are being wrapped.'

Borsini bowed and said, 'I look forward to resuming our lessons soon, *signorina. Buongiorno.*'

As soon as we were alone, Weylin said, 'You had my note?'

'Yes. I am surprised to see you dawdling about the shops. I thought you would be looking for Andrew. Mama is very eager to meet him.'

'I have hired a man to trace Jones. I am no sleuth. The job requires an expert.'

'That leaves you free to chaperon Borsini.'

'I happened to be free for an hour,' he said with a shrug.

'It did not occur to you to call at Hernefield?' I snipped. 'Mama was very upset at your note. It would have made it easier if you had come in person.'

'You showed her the letter, then? I was not sure you would want to worry her with the details.'

'Of course I showed it to her. She has a right to know.'

'I have not told Mama yet. I was waiting for a reply to my note before calling on you.'

Why had I not thought of that! I should have answered his note. 'Do you not plan to acknowledge Andrew, then?'

'That must depend on what sort of fellow he is. I shan't introduce a scoundrel into the house as a relation and friend.'

'I wish you will tell Mama so! She is refurbishing a guest room for him. She speaks of buying him a mount.'

Weylin stared in dismay. 'Good God!'

'Oh yes. She even speaks of allowing him a right to reside at Hernefield in her Will. I half hope he is a recognizable scoundrel, or she will disinherit me entirely.'

He laughed lightly. 'In that case, you must come to stay at Parham, Zoie. You will be home this evening?'

'Yes. Mama is having her cronies in for cards, but I only play when Mrs Vale cannot come. She is coming this evening. Shall I expect you to call?'

'That was my intention.'

Borsini rejoined us as the clerk brought out my parcel. 'Let me carry that to the carriage for you,' Borsini offered.

'You finish up your purchase, Borsini,' Weylin said. 'I shall escort Miss Barron.'

I looked for a hint of jealousy in Weylin's manner, but could find only impatience. Weylin carried the oils, the clerk carried the easel, and we three went out to the carriage. I was happy to know Weylin would call that evening, but still mystified by his dancing such assiduous attention on Borsini.

Only a few days ago he had scoffed at Borsini's claim of having been commissioned to paint the Prince Regent. He had spurned his artistic talent and questioned his title. Now suddenly he had not only commissioned Borsini to paint his mother, he had actually moved him into his house. And he had done it before going to the studio to judge the merit of his painting, too. I could only conclude Weylin had satisfied himself as to Borsini's right to his title. Or as this was so unlikely, I thought perhaps Lady Weylin had taken an unaccountable liking to the artist. She now had two pets to occupy her – Bubbums and Borsini.

Chapter Eighteen

My foolish pride enjoyed the idea of entertaining Lord Weylin in one corner of the saloon while Mama's friends played whist in the other. The old cats had begun teasing me about still being single. Last week, when I had been mending my stockings by the lamp table, Mrs Monroe, whose tongue is sharp as a bodkin, had jokingly asked if I was making myself a cap. Whatever Weylin's real motive in coming, the ladies would be in a frenzy to know if it was a courting call.

I took pains with my toilette. The Grecian gown was set aside for a more conservative gold lute-string, which cast a warm glow on my cheeks, and contrasted nicely with my black hair. I took a book of poetry to my usual chair beside the lamp, mentally admiring the artful picture I would present to Weylin when he was shown in.

The first disappointment was that Steptoe did not announce Lord Weylin wished to see Miss Barron. He came and hissed in my ear, 'His lordship is outside, wanting a word with you.'

'Pray send his lordship in, Steptoe,' I said, loudly enough that it might have been overheard at the card table, if Mrs Monroe had not been arguing in an auctioneer's voice about whose turn it was to serve.

'He wants a private word,' Steptoe said. 'When he heard the ladies cackling, he said, "We shan't disturb them. Is there a quiet corner somewhere, Steptoe?" I put them in the study.'

'Them? Who is with him?' The only person I could think of was Lady Weylin. That would be a feather in our cap indeed! The countess seldom stirred from her sofa.

'Count Borsini,' Steptoe hissed.

How were we to have any private conversation with Borsini present? Surely Weylin had not told Borsini about Andrew Jones! My poetic smile had dwindled to a scowl when I followed Steptoe from the saloon and into the study.

I found the gentlemen in the jumbled little study, the worst room in the house. Mama had removed the double-pedestal desk to Andrew's room, as threatened. In its place sat a poky, battered table that hardly had room for the writing pad and three inkpots. The only seating was four wooden chairs.

As soon as we exchanged greetings, I said, 'I cannot imagine why Steptoe put you in here. The place is a mess. Mama is just rearranging the furniture. Let us go into the saloon.'

'This looks perfectly comfortable,' Weylin lied, and showed me to one of the wooden chairs, before taking one himself. I daresay he read the question in my eyes, for his next speech concerned Borsini. 'Mama retired early. I could not leave Borsini rattling around the house alone.'

'You have prepared your canvas for the portrait, have you, Borsini?' I asked civilly, to suggest what other occupation he might have found for himself.

'I put the gesso on it this afternoon. It is all ready to go,' he replied.

The three of us sat staring at one another like strangers at a coach stop, waiting for a carriage. 'Would you care for a glass of wine?' I said, to break the silence.

They agreed, and I rang for Steptoe. The wine was brought and drunk, with very little conversation. As we could not speak of Andrew, the talk turned to painting. Borsini described the pose and costume he would use to paint Lady Weylin. I was not surprised to learn she would be painted lounging on her chaise longue, with Bubbums at her feet.

'That should look very natural,' I said.

Weylin's lips moved in amusement, though I did not mean any offence. 'Borsini was telling me you two met in Brighton,' he said.

'Yes, a few years ago,' I agreed. Weylin looked surprised.

'Five years ago,' Borsini said.

'Was it really that long ago? My uncle was with us, so it cannot have been more than five years.'

'Your uncle had just returned from India,' Borsini reminded me. 'Do you not recall he wanted his portrait taken, but decided to wait until his complexion had faded somewhat?'

'Yes, I believe you are right. How time flies.' But not tonight. The visit seemed to drag on endlessly and boringly.

Borsini inquired once again about the progress of my studio, and I repeated that I was satisfied with the color.

'Perhaps I could see it?' he suggested.

Happy for anything to do, I stood up to take him abovestairs. He said, 'Steptoe will show me up. There is no need for you to disturb yourself.'

'Let us all go,' Weylin said at once, just when I hoped for a few moments alone with him.

'There is nothing to see,' I assured him. 'Borsini just wants to check on the color of the walls.'

'I shan't be a moment,' Borsini said, and disappeared through the door.

As soon as he was gone, Weylin said, 'Do you think it wise to let Borsini upstairs alone?'

'He is not alone. Steptoe is with him.'

'All the worse!'

'What do you mean?'

'Steptoe called at Parham this afternoon. He did not actually come to the door, but sent a note. Borsini met him in the meadow. I happened to see them from my bedroom window. It happened shortly after we returned from Aldershot.'

'Steptoe pestering Borsini? What is the wretch up to now?'

'I haven't the least notion. But when I mentioned to Mama that I was coming here, Borsini pitched himself into coming with me, without the least encouragement from me. This sudden enthusiasm to see the studio – it could be a ruse to have a private word with Steptoe.'

'Then let us sneak up behind them and listen!'

We darted out of the study. At the end of the hall, I noticed the door to the butler's little room was ajar. No one was visible, but the shadows of two men were cast on the floor. Weylin took a step forward. I held him back. 'Go quietly!'

We tiptoed closer. Steptoe was speaking in a low, urgent voice. 'I tell you I saw it with my own eyes.'

Borsini asked, 'When? How long ago?'

'Just before he died. I have ransacked the house since then, looking for it. I fear he destroyed it.'

'He would never do that. There is a fiver in it for you if you find it and bring it to me.'

'A fiver!' Steptoe jeered. 'Make it a hundred and you've got yourself a deal, mate.'

'Very well, a hundred. Let us go above and look for it.'

We leapt away from the door as the shadows moved. When they came out of the room, I said, as though surprised, 'Borsini! You have not gone up to the studio after all. Lord Weylin and I had decided to join you. You may stay here, Steptoe, in case Mama needs you.'

155

Borsini looked as guilty as a cat with cream on his whiskers. Steptoe, more hardened in crime, just scowled. They had no alternative but to go along with my suggestion, however. I got a lamp and took the gentlemen up to glance a moment at the walls of the studio. One could get very little idea of the color at night, by the light of one lamp.

'I should return tomorrow, in daylight,' Borsini said. Behind his back, Weylin lifted his eyebrows at this suggestion.

'Perhaps that would be best,' I agreed.

We all went back downstairs to the study. The visit was over, and Mama's card partners had not even seen Weylin. He gave me a meaningful look and said, 'You recall I was to have a word with your mama, Zoie. I shall just leave a note for her. You will see that she gets it.' He disappeared into the study a moment, and handed me the note when he returned.

His eyes told me the note was for me. I accompanied them to the entrance, Steptoe saw them out, and I returned to the saloon to read my note.

He had jotted only one sentence. 'Meet me in your rose garden in thirty minutes.' A tingle of anticipation trembled through me. For twenty-five minutes I sat gazing at the poetry book, while my mind roamed far and wide over this new mystery. Borsini was looking for something in this house. Something that was worth a hundred pounds to him. Something that Steptoe had seen before Uncle Barry died. What possible interest could Borsini have in my uncle?

I could only think the 'something' was an item Borsini could turn into cash and Steptoe could not, or Steptoe would keep the item for himself. That left out jewelry or any fancy bibelot Barry had picked up in India. Or was it something that cast a doubt on Borsini's character, or even identity? His papa's palazzo had a way of roaming about Italy. Perhaps my uncle had chanced

156

across something that did discredit to the artist. A piece in the paper announcing he had been arrested? There had been several occasions when Borsini had to cancel our lesson. Had he sold forged pictures as originals, or ruined a highly born daughter he was giving lessons to? Any of these was possible. It would explain Borsini working in a small town like Aldershot, where he did not meet anyone important. That had always seemed strange to me.

In twenty-five minutes I went to the library, to slip out by the side door into the rose garden. I noticed then that Steptoe was not on duty. He had certainly gone upstairs to have a look for whatever it was Borsini wanted. I did not think it likely he would find it. Whatever it was, he had been looking for it ever since Barry's death.

I went to the kitchen and asked Brodagan to find Steptoe and see that he returned to his duties, as Mama might want him at any time.

'I know where he'll be, melady, for he spends more time in them trunks of your uncle's old clothes than the moths do. He is up to something, the twisty creature.'

'Lock the attic door, Brodagan, and do not let Steptoe up there under any circumstances.'

'Aye, and I'll hide the ladder in the shed, or he'll break a window and fly in like a bat.'

I turned to leave, but she stopped me with a complaint. 'Do you see what poor sort of a cake I have to put on the table for melady's guests? Didn't it rise up light as a cloud, but when that gossoon of a Jamie dropped a big log on the floor, the cake fell till it looks like an omelet.'

The cake was a good six inches high. 'It looks fine.'

'Fine, is it? I am ashamed to put it on the table. It looked fine before Jamie dropped the log. There's six eggs and two cups of flour wasted. I only hope melady's guests are hungry enough to eat it.'

'It's lovely.'

I escaped, before she could start on the inadequacies of the cold cuts and bread, and hastened to the rose garden.

Chapter Nineteen

The night was warm and balmy. Moonbeams cast a wan light on the garden, bleaching the pink and yellow roses to white, and turning the bushes a sinister black. As if to make up for stealing the garden's color, night enhanced its perfume. The very attar of roses hung heavy on the air. On such a night did Romeo beguile his way to Juliet's balcony. My attention was diverted by the sound of hoofbeats from the park. A dark shadow appeared over a rise of ground. It advanced swiftly, revealing itself as Weylin, mounted on his black gelding, coming to me by moonlight. A lady would have to be withered and sere not to feel a frisson of anticipation at such a sight.

I went forward to meet him. He hopped down from his horse, wearing not a romantic smile but a scowl.

'I should have given myself longer than half an hour,' he said, breathing heavily. 'I had the devil of a time getting away from Borsini. What must the clunch do but go to the stable, to say good night to that spavined jade of his.'

'There was no hurry,' I assured him.

He dropped onto a stone bench to recover his breath. I sat beside him and said, 'The roses smell lovely, do they not?'

'I daresay. It is difficult to tell, with the scent of the stable – and on my good jacket, too.' He actually lifted his arm and sniffed at his sleeve.

This effectively destroyed the romantic mood of moonlight and roses. I said curtly, 'What do you make of Borsini and Steptoe sharing a secret, Weylin? I have been pondering it this half hour, and cannot make up my mind.'

'I have no proof, but I shall share my suspicions with you. I think it is Borsini who has been posing as my aunt's son, Andrew Jones.'

The notion was so bizarre, and so unexpected, that I emitted a snort of laughter. 'Why do you say posing as their son? Did the lawyer not have proof of it?'

'He has proof a son exists, but that is not to say the man visiting at Lindfield is the true son.'

'If that man was Borsini, he would hardly assume the persona of an Italian count. You recall Andrew Jones was found in Ireland, teaching in a boys' school.'

'Teaching *art*,' Weylin said, and wrinkled his brow, as if that proved anything.

'Barry's letter did not say art.'

'One of the letters mentioned it. You did not read them all. I have been over them with a fine-tooth comb. When did Borsini turn up in Brighton?' When he answered himself, I realized it had been a rhetorical question. 'Five years ago, shortly after your uncle arrived at Hernefield. Who introduced Borsini to you? Your uncle. I have weaseled this information out of Borsini. Is it not true that McShane met Borsini first?'

'Yes, it was my uncle who took Mama and me to his exhibition, but—'

He lifted an imperious hand to silence me. 'But me no buts until I have finished, Zoie. I have already conned all your objections. I believe I can answer them. Here is what I think happened.

Your uncle knew long ago, before he ever left Ireland, that Margaret was enceinte. He made it his business to learn that the child was put out for adoption. When he returned from India a quarter of a century later, virtually penniless—'

'He had five thousand pounds.'

'That is hardly enough to retire comfortably – but it was enough to hire Borsini to pose as his and my aunt's long-lost son, and diddle her out of her fortune.'

'This is a monstrous accusation!' Yet I remembered Steptoe's sly grin, and his talk of Barry and Jones being involved in criminal doings. Steptoe knew Borsini was Jones, and had gone up to Parham to threaten or bargain with him.

'Hear me out! Your uncle came to England; then, hot on his heels, Count Borsini appears at Brighton. Your uncle takes you to Brighton, to his studio. Within months, Borsini suddenly transfers his business to Aldershot – hardly the art mecca of Europe! Matters are arranged in such a manner that Borsini is a regular visitor at Hernefield, where he and your uncle can connive at their scheme. Lady Margaret is an ageing, lonely, well-dowered lady, eager to believe she has found her long-lost son. I doubt she conducted any strenuous inquiries into Borsini's past.'

I listened in astonishment to this outlandish story. Yet there was enough truth in it to pique my interest. 'You have not explained how this English bastard ended up as an Italian nobleman. Are we to believe the real Count Borsini is a part of this plot?'

'There is no Count Borsini. They got the name from a wine bottle. Borsini is as Irish as poteen. He has the typical looks of the black Irish. He knows half a dozen Italian words, and imitates the accent, to cozen the ladies. Your uncle probably did find him teaching at a school in Ireland. He had to come from somewhere.'

'You're mad. Why would Borsini pose as an Italian at all? That was an unnecessary complication.'

'That was to divert suspicion. Who would ever connect an Italian count to McShane or Lady Margaret? Borsini was in close contact with you and your mama. You would not look for a resemblance to your uncle if you believed him a foreigner.'

'No, and we would not find any resemblance if we looked till the cows came home.'

'He has dark hair like McShane, and blue eyes like Margaret. I don't know whether Margaret was aware of the double life of Borsini. He says he never met her, but even if he did, he would say it was a pose to allow father and son to meet without arousing suspicion.'

'If my uncle conned your aunt out of her fortune, how does it come he died penniless?' I demanded.

'I can only assume he was a demmed poor manager. His Indian career supports the theory. I daresay Borsini ended up with the lot. I don't claim to know all the details. They may have had a safety box, each having keys. Whichever died first, the other got the money.'

'There is not much doubt which would die first. My uncle was an old man. Why would he go to all the trouble of bilking your aunt, and go on living like a pauper, just to hand the money over to a stranger? If there is any shred of truth in this unlikely tale – and I don't believe it for a moment – then Borsini is their real son.'

'That is another possibility. I had quite convinced myself of it – until Steptoe entered the picture. You recall this evening Borsini displayed an unholy eagerness to get into your late uncle's room to look for something. Something he did not wish us to see.'

'And what would this item be? A deathbed confession written by my uncle?' I asked satirically.

'Hardly that, I think. More likely they had a written agreement of some sort. Or perhaps letters relating to the scheme. The possibilities are endless. The missing item might be a key to a safety box. That would explain why it is of value to Borsini, who knows where the box is, and useless to Steptoe.'

'I thought Borsini and Barry both had a key to this imaginary safety box.'

'Borsini may have lost his, I am just suggesting possibilities.'

'I have noticed you are quick to suggest any possibility that makes my uncle into an ogre and a thief.'

'Cut line, Zoie. I learned, in London, why your uncle retired early. Funds missing from the EIC, was it not? You are defending the indefensible.'

'You have been checking up on my uncle? Dragging our name through the mud! My uncle did not steal that money. One of his underlings took it. He told us all about it. They caught the man, and got the money back. My uncle retired voluntarily, with his full pension. They would not have given him his pension if he had robbed them.'

'They got a part of the money back. McShane was in charge. He was either involved, or a demmed bad manager, as I said. Demme, I don't see why you are so angry. I am not suggesting McShane's character reflects in any way on you. He conned you and your mama. No disgrace in being a victim. Every family has its dirty dishes. My own Cousin Albert embezzled a fortune from his friends on forged mining stocks. Scratch any rich man and you will find a scoundrel; if not in the present generation, you do not have to go far back in history. I thought we were working on this together.'

'No, Weylin. It is clear to me you are working to turn your aunt into one of those innocent victims, to my uncle's discredit.'

'You won't admit Borsini is a crook, in other words,' he said.

'That is what this is all about. You have fallen for his smooth lies. I have heard him at work on Mama. I know how he operates. Never has he seen such lustrous eyes, such a complexion, like rose petals. Can she really hear, with those dainty ears, like seashells? The man is nothing but a gigolo. I shall kick him out the door as soon as we find this item he and Steptoe are looking for. And I'll have back my aunt's fortune as well, to give to her real son.'

'You don't know that Borsini is not the real son,' I said. I would have said more, were it not for those familiar old compliments. I daresay Lady Weylin would be pulling her hair back in a Grecian knot and donning a toga before long.

I kept remembering, too, how well Borsini and Uncle Barry got along together. In the inclement weather, I used to send the carriage to Aldershot for him. As often as not, Barry would go along for the ride. I had thought he was just bored in his retirement, but now I began to wonder.

Every few months, Borsini would miss a lesson. I had taken no special note of the times, but it did seem to be about once a quarter. He had missed the lessons because he had been at Tunbridge Wells, posing as Andrew Jones. The timing of Borsini's entry into my life, and the fact that it was Barry who introduced us . . .

Weylin said, 'If Borsini is their son, why does he not say so? And why is he looking for that certain something, offering to pay a hundred pounds for it? That is not the behavior of an innocent man, Zoie.'

'If there is anything in this house to prove it, I shall find it, if I have to tear down the walls and pull up the floorboards.'

'I shall come over early tomorrow morning. The place to begin is in your uncle's room.'

'My uncle used the octagonal tower – that is now my studio. It has been stripped bare. His personal effects were taken to the attic. Mama and I – and Steptoe – have been through them a dozen times.'

We sat a moment, pondering this problem. Weylin said, 'There is more than one way to skin a cat. Borsini has a past, and we won't have to go all the way to Italy to discover it. I shall send a man to Dublin to check into this boys' school. There will be some record of a teacher leaving unexpectedly five years ago. I daresay he has a full set of parents of his own, and a birth document to prove it. But first we'll have one more go at the studio, and the attics.'

Something in me disliked to see my old friend Borsini disgraced. I knew his charm was only a second-rate thing. I had never really believed the palazzo in Venice, or the vineyards, but he had been kind and thoughtful in his way. He used to bring little bouquets of violets in the spring, and say he wished they were orchids. He always remembered any personal thing I told him. When I said I liked Thomas Grey, he had got a copy of his poems at the circulating library and read them. He used to send a card on my birthday, with a poem so awful, I knew without being told that he had written it himself.

He had always been respectful to me. There had been several occasions when he might have made improper advances. He always behaved like the perfect gentleman. His compliments on complexion and ears were given shyly, while he worked. I knew they were like cologne, to be sniffed and enjoyed, not taken seriously. He never once touched me in any familiar way. Other than the occasional mention of the family estate in Italy, he was modest and unassuming. If he was a thief, it was my uncle who had seduced him into it. I could not like to see poor Borsini take the brunt of it, and that was exactly what Weylin had in mind.

'You need not trouble yourself to come and search, Weylin,' I said, and stood up to leave. 'I shall do it myself.'

Weylin rose and looked at me through eyes narrowed to slits. 'And conceal the evidence?' he said. 'You are letting your partiality for Borsini lead you astray.'

'He is not a bad man, whatever you say.'

I did not expect such an outburst. Weylin flew into a towering rage. 'So he has been sweet-talking you all the while, has he? Oozing his pseudo-Latin charm on you. Has he screwed himself to the sticking point? Or have you, like my aunt, given yourself without benefit of marriage?'

When I figured out what he meant, I lost the last vestige of control. I raised my hand and struck him a resounding blow on the cheek. The slap echoed on the still night air, with Weylin's gasp of surprise coming after it, the echo of an echo.

'How dare you! I'll have you know, Lord Weylin, Count Borsini is a gentleman. He may not have any right to his title, and he may not have a family mansion behind him, but he—'

'Are you engaged to him?' he said, cutting into my tirade. 'You have lost your mind, Zoie. When an engagement must be kept under wraps, that should be enough to tell you there is something wrong with it.'

'I am not engaged to him! He has never touched me – in that way, I mean. We are friends.'

I watched as the fury subsided to anger, and softened further to embarrassment. 'I am happy to hear it,' he said, quite mildly. 'I admit I rather liked him myself before—'

'Before you took the notion he was posing as Andrew Jones?'

'Oh no. I suspected that earlier, which is why I took him to Parham, to pick his brains a little.' He stood, looking ill at ease, a completely new posture for Lord Weylin. 'I am sorry if I offended you, Zoie.'

'And I am sorry I attacked you, but I am not accustomed to being accused of loose and wanton behavior. It strikes me you have a poor notion of my character, sir. First you thought I was stealing that stupid little pot at Parham.'

'A Ming vase!'

'I didn't know that, did I? We have one exactly like it in our spare room.'

'Not exactly like it, I think. You have your blind spots as well, you see.' His hands rose and seized my wrists. 'Why do you think I flew into a pelter when you leapt to Borsini's defence?' he said, in a husky voice. His fingers eased up my forearms until they were holding me in a tight grip, and all the while his head was inching slowly to mine, as if drawn by an inexorable force.

My throat felt swollen. When I spoke, my voice had that same choked sound as Weylin's. 'I do not see it is any of your business,' I said weakly.

'Blind as the proverbial bat,' he said softly, and seized my lips for a scalding kiss, there in the moonlight, with the cloying scent of roses around us – and just a whiff of the stable, too, from his jacket. Weylin was no uncertain, teenaged Romeo. He did not woo like a babe, but like a fully grown man. I felt the passion in him, and was aware of an answering force rising like a tide inside me, matching every pressure of body and lips. His arms pressed me against his hard chest, and my hands found their way to his neck. My fingers moved possessively through his crisp hair.

He moved one hand to rest against my throat, the fingers splayed so they touched my shoulder. His moving fingers felt fevered. I could feel my pulse throb against them with every beat of my heart. A heat grew between us; flames licked along my veins and rose in a delirium to my head, robbing me of sense.

Was this how Lady Margaret had lost her virtue? I did not know whether she deserved pity or envy. Through the swirling mist of passion, I remembered Weylin's hint that I had given myself to Borsini. Weylin had made no declaration of love, or of honorable intention. Was he trifling with me? I felt my body stiffen involuntarily. The heat cooled to a chilling anger. I pulled away and glared at him.

'Don't look at me like that!' he said gruffly. 'If I got a little carried away, it was not all my doing, Zoie.'

I waited to hear the more interesting words I had been hoping for. When they did not come, I said coolly, 'You had best go now, Weylin.'

'There is no hurry.' He tried to pull me back into his arms. I stepped back with a twitch of my skirts.

He said, 'What time shall I come in the morning?'

'I shall let you know if I discover anything.'

'Nine o'clock. I shall be here at nine.' He looked all around the garden, inhaling the scent of roses. Then he looked up at the moon and smiled. 'It seems a shame to waste that moon,' he said, with a quizzing smile.

I was ready to blame the moon for half my behavior. 'It will light your way home,' I told him.

He stood a moment, looking at me in an assessing way. My stiff demeanor told him the lovemaking was over. He accepted it, whistled for his mount, and left with a wave.

I went back inside, determined to be in the attic by seven o'clock tomorrow morning for a private search. And I would have Brodagan or Mama come upstairs with us when Weylin arrived at nine, if I had no luck before that, to keep him in line.

I returned to my lamp chair and my book of poetry, to review our meeting in the garden. How Mrs Monroe would stare if she knew what brought that smile to my face! Put on my caps indeed! Put on a tiara was more like it. That embrace in the garden told me Weylin loved me, and I meant to see that he did the proper thing about it.

Chapter Twenty

Despite my intention, I did not have a root through the attic
trunks before Weylin's arrival the next morning after all.
Brodagan came down with a toothache in the night, and when
Brodagan has the toothache, they hear of it in Scotland and Wales.
Morpheus himself could not sleep for the moaning. Servants
raced through the halls bringing her oil of cloves and camphor,
tincture of myrrh and friar's balsam and brandy – all to no avail.
When it became clear that this was one of Brodagan's major
toothaches, as opposed to the minor ones that cure themselves
after a toothful of brandy, I knew my duty, and I did it.

I got out of bed at two o'clock in the morning and went belowstairs to prepare her a posset with a few drops of laudanum, to let
the poor soul rest. I would insist she have that distressed tooth
removed in the morning. Steptoe came to the kitchen to inquire
what was amiss. He was wearing a dressing gown that belonged
to a dandified lord. It was green silk with gold tassels on the belt.
On the pocket some family crest was embroidered. Either
Pakenham's or Weylin's, no doubt. I told him of Brodagan's trouble. He stirred up the moldering embers in the stove, and between
us we got the milk heated. There was enough for two, and I took
the pan with me, planning to have the second cup myself, without

the laudanum. I added a few drops of the medicine to Brodagan's cup and went upstairs.

Brodagan lay in bed with a hot brick against her cheek, cushioned with a wad of flannelette. Without her headpiece, and with her face shriveled in pain, she looked no more formidable than young Mary. Mary was with her, warming another brick at the grate, to replace the one in use when it cooled off.

'My sharp grief,' Brodagan sighed from the pillow. 'I'll not keep this tooth in my head another day, melady, not if they offer me honey on dishes.'

'I have made you a posset, Brodagan,' I said. 'I want you to drink it up, and get some sleep. Tomorrow you must have that infected tooth removed.' During the throes of an attack, she always agreed to this, but as soon as the pain eased, she reverted to her claim that if God had meant her to gum her victuals, he would not have put teeth in her head.

'I'll take the hard end of the matter and have it out this time, though it be the end of me,' she moaned. 'Why is God doing me such a wrong? I never oppressed a flea in my life.'

Mary blessed herself at this questioning of the Almighty. Our servants are all Papists. Brodagan sighed and sipped the posset. 'Lie down and get a wink of sleep if you can, Mary,' she said weakly, 'for you'll have all the toil of the kitchen on your back tomorrow.' Mary refused to budge. 'The girl is an angel to her toes, melady. If her heart was on fire, she'd not leave me in my distress.'

'Drink it all up,' I said, holding the cup to her lips until the glass was empty. 'You can run along, Mary. I shall stay with Brodagan until she sleeps.'

She soon grew drowsy. Mary replaced the cooling brick with a hot one and finally left. I poured myself the other cup of posset and took it to my room. The hot milk was as good as a sleeping draft, and soon I was sleeping as soundly as Brodagan.

And that is why I did not awaken until nearly nine o'clock in the morning. I was just entering the breakfast parlour when Weylin was shown in. His bright eye told me he had enjoyed a good night's sleep. I studied him for any other tacit messages, and thought I detected a trace of admiration as well.

'Borsini is busy with Mama's portrait,' he said. 'He hinted to know where I was going when I left the house. I told him I had some business to attend to. He will think I have gone to Aldershot.'

I stifled a yawn into my fist and said, 'Oh.'

Weylin examined me with a worried frown. 'You look like the wrath of God, Zoie. Have you spent the entire night searching the attics?'

'No, tending to Brodagan's toothache.'

'You have my condolences. I am familiar with the phenomenon. An Irish toothache is like an Irish wake. More sound and fury than a war. By the by, I notice Steptoe keeps bankers' hours. He did not answer the door.'

This was nothing new, but when Mary brought coffee, I asked her to please tell Steptoe I wished a word with him.

Mary blinked in surprise. 'Why, Steptoe has left, melady. We thought you had given him his marching papers, for his room is empty and his clothes gone. Brodagan said if she wasn't at death's door, she'd rise up and dance a jig for joy.'

'What! Steptoe gone!' I exclaimed.

Both Weylin and myself jumped to our feet in alarm.

'He's gone, miss, but I counted the silver, and he didn't take anything with him, as far as I can tell – except that all the kitchen candles are missing.'

'By God, he's found it!' Weylin exclaimed.

'I asked Brodagan to lock the attic door,' I said.

Mary gaped at us as if we had suddenly begun speaking in

tongues. I asked her to see how Brodagan was doing, and she left. Without another word, Weylin and I bolted upstairs. The attic door was not only unlocked, but hung ajar. We darted up the narrow stairway, into a scene of chaos. Barry's trunks had been dragged from the wall into the middle of the room, for easier searching. The contents were flung about at random. The jackets had the lining ripped out. A dozen candles had been arranged in a circle around the trunks, giving the scene a mystical air. They had burned low, indicating a long burning, but at least he had extinguished them before leaving. I sighed wearily, and Weylin uttered a few words never spoken in church.

'Just when I thought Steptoe was beginning to shape up,' I scowled. 'He was quite helpful last night when I was making Brodagan's posset. I should have been suspicious that he was awake at two o'clock in the morning. How did he get up here? Brodagan locked the door, and she had the only key.'

I picked up a ripped jacket, and there on the floor beneath it sat Brodagan's key ring, with the brass shamrock she carries for good luck.

'How did he get hold of this? It was in Brodagan's room.' Even as I spoke, I realized his ruse. 'He knew I was preparing her laudanum. He went into her room and stole the keys, bold as brass, while she slept soundly.' I wondered if he had sneaked a few drops into my own milk as well. That would account for my deep sleep, but I did not mention that. 'Borsini is still at Parham, you say?'

'Yes, and Steptoe has not visited, for I have Borsini watched around the clock. He did not stir from the house last night.'

'They might be meeting now! Go back to Parham. You'll catch them red-handed.'

'If they are meeting, I'll know about it. As I said, Borsini is watched.'

I just shook my head in confusion. 'At least we are rid of Steptoe once and for all. He won't have the gall to show his nose here after this.'

Weylin said, 'Let us have a look around his room. He may have left something to tell us where he was going.'

I led him to Steptoe's room. Steptoe had packed hastily, leaving half his clothes behind. We searched them for clues, but of course, he was too crafty to leave anything but lint in the pockets.

'This is the dressing gown he was wearing last night,' I said, lifting the green robe, which had been tossed on the end of the bed in his haste. 'Quite the peacock! I wonder where he stole this.'

'Peacock?' Weylin said, offended. He took the garment and examined it. 'He told my valet this got grease spilled on it when it was sent down to be pressed. I shall have a word with my valet about this.' He frowned at the garment. 'Perhaps it is just a tad gaudy,' he said sheepishly. 'The yellow trim is the culprit.'

'Let us go downstairs and have some coffee. I was just about to have breakfast when you arrived.'

We went below and found Mama at the breakfast table. 'Mary told me about Steptoe,' she said. 'Did you find anything interesting abovestairs?'

Weylin said only that Steptoe and Borsini appeared to be in league in some mischief, without mentioning Barry, and told her of Steptoe's depredations in the attic.

'I am shocked at Borsini,' she said. 'He always seemed such a nice lad, except for that foreign streak, of course. I never could get used to being a *signora*. And you say Steptoe planned to sell what he found to Borsini?'

'For a hundred pounds,' I said.

'If it was something small enough to be hidden in the lining of a jacket, it sounds like a piece of paper,' Mama said. 'Whatever

173

could it be? Something to poor Borsini's discredit, I don't doubt. Steptoe could mail it to him.'

Weylin set down his cup with a clatter and jumped up. 'You're right. And the mail will be arriving any moment. I must go.'

I did not think Steptoe would part with the item without getting his hundred pounds in his hand, but Weylin tore out of the house. Mama and I remained behind to talk over the matter. This was done in a vague way, as I did not want to tell her my suspicions of Barry. We discussed whether we should send for the constable. Since Steptoe had not stolen anything, and had, in fact, run off with a month's wages owing to him, we could not see what charges we could lay against him.

'Whatever he is up to, we are well rid of him,' she said.

The next item of business was to get Brodagan shipped off to the tooth-drawer. The pain had eased, and she was in no mind to part with her tooth, but in the end we bullocked her into it.

'I shall go with you, Brodagan,' Mama said. 'You will not be alone in your agony.'

I made sure I would have the chore of escorting Brodagan, and wondered at Mama pitching herself into such an unpleasant situation. I soon found the reason.

'You will know what to tell the constable when Weylin has Borsini arrested, Zoie,' Mama said. 'They are bound to come here asking questions, as you and Borsini were such bosom bows. It will be better if you handle it. You will know what to say.'

I felt I got the better of the bargain. I would rather face a den of lions than Brodagan at the tooth-drawer's. In honor of the occasion, Brodagan wore a freshly starched steeple, with a voluminous black cape over her shoulders, though the weather was warm. She was supported by Mama's arm on one side, Mary's on the other, as she went moaning through the hall.

She stopped at the door and took one last look around. 'In case

I never see you again, melady, I'll take my leave of you now,' she said to me, in sonorous accents. 'It has been an honor to serve you.' I gave her a parting hug.

Mary said bracingly, 'Why you'll be back before you can say one, two, three, with that malign tooth out of your head once and for all, and your heart light as a thrush.'

'Light as a thrush, is it?' Brodagan said. 'I only hope it's light enough to fly to heaven.'

'Here, have a sip of your medicine,' Mary said, and handed her a little bottle of brandy she had brought along to brace Brodagan for her ordeal.

With Steptoe, Brodagan, Mama, Mary, and John Groom gone, the house was left with only Jamie, the backhouse boy, and myself. I should have asked Mama to bring one of the Coughlin girls home to help out. They are local girls who work mornings at a dairy farm, but are always glad to find extra work for the afternoon.

I went to the kitchen, where Jamie was piling dishes into the wash pan. He seemed to know what he was about, so I left him to it and went back upstairs. I would sit in the saloon to act as butler. Rather than twiddling my thumbs, I went upstairs to fetch my sketchpad and pencils. I noticed the door to the octagonal tower was ajar. Steptoe! If he had done any damage to my studio, I would call the constable.

I ran upstairs, but the room had not been disturbed. Sunlight spilling in at the windows glowed on the light walls. I could not complain of any lack of brightness. Quite the contrary. My two easels and chest of paints and brushes had been brought up. The easels lay on the floor, the parcel of supplies on the chest of drawers. The painters had removed their tarpaulin, revealing the aged Persian rug. I could not remove it by myself, but I could measure the room for its new matting covering. I stood a moment,

175

wondering what color would suit. Perhaps a darker shade, to conceal the inevitable spatters of paint, and to give some relief from those brilliant walls and windows.

Yet in winter, the windows would show a grey sky, so perhaps . . . What I really wanted was to ask Borsini's opinion. I would miss my old friend and mentor. I could not believe he was in league with that hound of a Steptoe. I could believe he really was Barry's son. That would have pleased me greatly – but then, how did Steptoe fit into such an innocent scenario as that?

While I stood in the stillness of the tower room, I heard from below soft, stealthy footsteps along the hallway. It was not Jamie's quick feet, but a man's tread, moving quietly, as if he had no right to be there. My heart clenched in fear. I was alone in the house, but for Jamie, in the kitchen below. He could not know the man had entered, or he would have notified me. This intruder had got in uninvited. Steptoe . . . or worse – a stranger. A ne'er-do-well who thought the house deserted, and had come to see what he could pick up. When he saw me, he might lose his mind and attack.

The soft steps proceeded down the hall. I heard a few doors open, then the steps came closer, and stopped. My ears suggested he was at my bedroom. After a moment, the footsteps began again, faster now, heading for the stairs to this tower room. I crouched behind the chest of drawers while the footsteps mounted swiftly, no longer using caution, almost as if he knew he had me cornered alone up here. My throat ached from the strain, and my heart banged erratically. There was not a single thing I could use for a weapon.

The footsteps ran into the room. 'Zoie! *Zoie!*' a voice called, rising in alarm. It was Weylin!

I stood up then, my fear giving way to anger. 'Weylin! What the devil do you mean, sneaking about the house like a burglar! You frightened the life out of me.'

176

'Zoie?' His face was white with strain. There was an answering anger in his tone. 'Why are you hiding? Why did no one answer the door? I knew Steptoe was gone and Brodagan *hors de combat*, so I let myself in. I called and called, without an answer. I could not imagine what had happened. I was afraid you had all been poisoned, or had your throats slit. Are you all right?'

'Of course I am all right.'

'But where is everyone? You were not alone when I left half an hour ago.'

I explained about Mama and Mary taking Brodagan to the dentist's, and of course, he already knew of Steptoe's departure.

'I shall send a few girls over from Parham,' he said. 'And a footman. Your mama should not have left you here alone. You are as white as a sheet. I don't feel any too stout myself. Let us go below and have a glass of wine.'

'A good idea. I just came up to get my sketchpad and pencils. My studio door was ajar. I feared Steptoe had been up, but if he was, he did not find anything. All my uncle's things have been removed.'

'I wonder . . .' He looked all around the room. 'We do not know for certain that Steptoe found what he was looking for. Is it possible McShane hid it in this room? Under a loose floorboard, or slid down the wainscoting?' He looked at the shabby old rug. 'Or under that? Of course, you would have looked there.'

My interest quickened. 'No, actually, the painters had the tarpaulin over this precious floor covering, to prevent splattering it.'

Weylin glanced to see if I was joking. 'No doubt Steptoe has had a peek,' he said, looking a question at me.

'I want to remove it in any case. Will you help me?'

We each took a corner and began rolling. The paper was right under the middle of the rug. I have no doubt Steptoe had lifted the corners as high as he could and peered under, missing the paper by inches. We both saw it at once, and reached for it. I beat Weylin to it by a second. The ink was faded, but still legible. We took it to the window to read. It was a marriage certificate, dated 1790, from St Agnes's Church in Duleek, Ireland. The signatures were Barry McShane and Lady Margaret Raleigh. The witnesses were Laurence McShane, a cousin of Barry's, and Mrs Riddle, Lady Margaret's companion. We examined the document in silence, then looked at each other in perplexity.

'But how is this possible?' I exclaimed. 'Your aunt was married to Mr MacIntosh.'

'I believe it is called bigamy,' Weylin said, in a choked voice. 'The old devil! And here I have been calling your uncle a scoundrel for having abandoned her.'

'I don't understand. If they were married, why did she not go to India with him, especially as she was having his child? This makes no sense, Weylin.'

'Aunt Margaret hated the heat,' he said. 'Chilly old Scotland suited her down to the toes. I wager she balked at the last minute.'

'Then she cannot have known she was enceinte.'

'Yes, that might explain – though not forgive it. She thought she could talk McShane out of going to India.'

'And he probably thought she would follow him. Mama always said he was mule-stubborn.'

'I daresay she was afraid to tell her papa what she had done – married your uncle, I mean. Grandpa Weylin was a Turk, with lofty ambitions for his daughters. So she got an offer from MacIntosh, and married him up in a hurry to escape to Scotland, to hide her sins from the family. I fancy that is what happened.'

'I wonder when Barry discovered all this. It must have been much later, after he had taken Surinda Joshi as his mistress.' Weylin looked a little startled at this. 'He kept an Indian woman for years in Calcutta. Mama was always afraid he would marry her. Now we know why he did not.'

We took the document down to the saloon and had a glass of wine. After much discussion, I said, 'This is all very interesting, but is this marriage certificate what Borsini and Steptoe were looking for? If Borsini is the legitimate son, he would not want to hide the fact. Quite the contrary. And if he is not, but only an impostor ... well, the marriage certificate hardly makes any difference.'

'If Lady Margaret was not MacIntosh's legitimate wife, then she has no right to her widow's portion. It will revert to MacIntosh's son. She handed the ten thousand over to the man she believed was her son, so he would certainly be eager to hide this little piece of paper.'

'Yes, I see what you mean. What should we do about it?'

'I shall have a word with Borsini. With this to hold over his head, he may be more forthcoming. I'll run along now. And for God's sake, Zoie, lock the door. I nearly had a heart attack when I thought you were dead.'

He sounded wonderfully worried. 'So did I, when I thought you were a burglar sneaking up on me. And I without a single weapon at hand to bludgeon you into submission.'

'No blunt instruments will be necessary. This will always keep me in line,' he said, and stole a quick kiss before parting.

Chapter Twenty-one

Brodagan returned home half an hour later with her steeple knocked askew and her face red from brandy and the tooth-drawer's mauling. She was smiling despite it all.

She held the offending tooth in her hand. 'I've lost my last night's sleep over this fellow, melady,' she said. 'To think such a wee scrap of bone could torture a body worse than the rack and thumbscrews. It's into the fire with Mr Snaggle Tooth, and good riddance, say I.' So saying, she tossed the offending article into the grate.

'Good for you, Brodagan. Was it very bad?' I asked.

'If hell has worse pain than a tooth-drawer, then I'll sin no more. I mean to get to heaven by hook or by crook.' She turned to Mama and said, 'I want to make a confession, melady. I didn't make dust rags out of that bit o' worn muslin off the blue guest room bed as you told me to, but made myself up a petticoat. It's been lying heavy on my conscience. I'll rip the petticoat up this very day and make it into dust rags, for a life of sin is not worth the torment.'

'Any worn muslin in this house is yours to do with as you see fit, Brodagan,' Mama said, with tears in her eyes. To me she added, 'Was ever a lady blessed with such honest servants, Zoie?

I swear they deserve halos, every one of them.'

Brodagan was much touched, and fell into tears. Mary joined in, and soon Mama was weeping as well. I felt a tear ooze out of my own eyes, and before we all drowned, we sent Brodagan off to bed. Mama went with her, which postponed telling her about Barry's having been married. She would be delighted to hear it, but the affair was so complicated that I wanted to ponder all its implications before telling her.

No, there is no point being evasive with you so late in my story. Like Brodagan, I shall confess the whole truth. I hoped to contrive some way for Andrew Jones (whom I believed to be Borsini) to keep his mama's fortune. Surely she had earned it. MacIntosh knew of her condition when he married her, and the fact that she was already married had not inconvenienced him much. His own son was already well provided for. Why should Andrew not have a piece of the pie? Mama might feel differently, however, so I would tread softly.

I was so upset that I could not settle down to painting or any other occupation, and decided to take a canter through the meadow to ease the tension. This would also give me a view of the Weylins' park. If anything of interest was transpiring, it was transpiring at Parham. All I saw was a couple of gardeners out scything the grass.

The major subject at luncheon was Brodagan's condition and our own shortage of servants. Brodagan's jaw was swollen up like a turnip. She wanted to work despite it; Mama forbade it; Mary and Jamie between them could hardly slice the mutton, much less cook it. The fire in the kitchen stove had gone out, and who was to answer the door if we had any callers? In the middle of our cold luncheon, the servants arrived from Parham. I had forgotten all about Weylin's offer to send them, but they were more than welcome.

Mama became tongue-tied in their presence. It was for me to
ask the footman to see to the stove, and assign the female servants
to Mary for instructions. As soon as lunch was over, Mama went
abovestairs to see that Mary had done the rooms, for she disliked
Weylin's servants to see the house dusty and the beds unmade.

'He knows we need help, Mama. That is why he sent his
servants to us.'

'Yes, dear, but servants from Parham! I would not want them
to think us slovenly.'

She went upstairs to make her own bed and dust her toilet
table. I sat by the window, waiting. It was not long before Weylin
and Borsini arrived. I do not know what caused it, but Borsini
had lost his second-rate air. He was wearing the same jacket, but
when he alit from Weylin's crested carriage, he walked with a
more confident air. He and Weylin might have come from the
same egg. That hint of obsequiousness that always hung about
him was gone. His head was held high and his shoulders were
straight. He looked as if he belonged in that carriage. He and
Weylin were talking and laughing like old friends.

I admitted them, as the footman was too busy tending to the
stove to act as butler. I knew by the mischievous light in Weylin's
eyes that he was happy about something. When Borsini came in,
he just smiled a moment from the doorway, then came forward,
put his arms around me, and kissed my cheek.

'Cousin!' He beamed. 'I have been wanting to call you that
these five years. Now you know the whole!'

'I still have a few questions,' I said, leading them to a seat, but
I was happy to hear Borsini was indeed my cousin, and not an
impostor.

'It is the money you are concerned about,' Borsini said. In the
past, he would not have been confident enough to put himself
forward in this manner. He would have waited for Weylin to

explain, or at least looked to him for permission. 'The fact of the matter is, that ten thousand pounds did not come from MacIntosh. It was Margaret's dowry. We do not see – Weylin and I – why it should go to Angus MacIntosh. He has more than enough.' He continued in this vein.

Although I listened closely (and agreed heartily), my eyes often strayed to Weylin. His composure told me he had accepted Borsini as his cousin. He read my unspoken question, and explained the reason.

'Andrew has proven to my satisfaction that he is Margaret's son. MacIntosh wanted him out of Scotland, and sent him to Ireland. He felt Andrew would feel at home there, since it was where his father was from. Andrew showed me the adoption papers and birth document the Joneses left him when they died. He knew he was adopted, but Mrs Jones told him he was the son of her cousin, who died in childbirth.'

'They were fine people,' Borsini said. 'Not well off, you know, but honest and hardworking. Mrs Jones was unable to have children. They are both dead now. In fact, they were getting on when they adopted me.'

'Andrew's life is chronicled from the beginning to the present,' Weylin said. 'He has his school diplomas from St Patrick's Academy in Dublin, and a letter of reference from the school where he taught. From the time he left there, we know where he was. First in Brighton, and later at Aldershot.'

'It was Barry's idea that I settle close to Hernefield,' Borsini added. 'I always called my real parents by their Christian names. To me, Mama and Papa are the folks who raised me. Margaret was afraid her secret would come out if we were seen together here, and approved Barry's idea of the little cottage near Ashdown Forest. Even there she insisted on hiding that we were all one family. In public, I was her nephew, and Barry was our butler, but of course, within the cottage we could be ourselves. We enjoyed some happy hours, telling each other all that had happened to us over the years. I thought you might tumble to it, Zoie, that my absence for a week every quarter coincided with your uncle's trips – ostensibly to London.'

'It never occurred to me. But why did you not tell us, Borsi—Andrew? You could have depended on Mama and myself to keep your secret.'

'Many's the time I was within a breath of it. It was Margaret who demanded secrecy, because of her bigamy. That is a serious crime.'

'Why did Margaret not go to India with Barry?' I asked. 'Did she know she was enceinte when he left?'

Andrew shook his head in frustration. 'I have heard them argue about it for hours on end. It was a challenge for power, cousin. She knew he had made arrangements to go to India when she married him. She thought she could convince him to stay in Ireland. He had no home to take her to, and was too proud to live off her money. He felt he could make his fortune in India. He was sure she would cave in and go with him at the last minute. He gave her an ultimatum: I am going. Meet me at the dock. She didn't show up, and he left without her. Neither of them knew that I was already more than a gleam in his eye.'

'That would have changed things, I daresay.'

'I like to think so,' he agreed. 'Shortly after Barry left, Margaret returned to England. When she discovered her condition, she panicked. Old Weylin was dead set against her marrying Barry. He wouldn't let him inside the door. They met at an assembly, and arranged trysts away from the house where she was visiting. Poor Margaret didn't know what to do. It seems MacIntosh had offered for her a year before. He showed up at Parham just when she was at her wits' end. She confided to him that she was enceinte, and he offered to marry her. What she did not tell him was that she was already married. She never did tell him. She wrote to Barry informing him what she had done, and said that if he told anyone of their marriage, she would kill herself. Since she had no idea where MacIntosh had sent me, Barry let the matter rest.'

'How did he find you then?' I asked.

'He read any English journals that came his way and eventually learned of MacIntosh's death. He thought Margaret would be in touch with him then, but years passed and she did not write. When there was that little trouble over the missing money Barry was completely innocent, and he proved it but he was unhappy in his work then, and decided to come back to England and try to straighten matters out. He paid a visit home to Ireland first, and while there, he heard of the Joneses having adopted a boy at about the time I was born. He traced me to the school where I was teaching art. You never saw any resemblance between us, Cousin, but I do look a little like him. Margaret says I have her eyes. Barry thought so, too. Well, the upshot of it was that he got in touch with Margaret, and her companion was able to provide the name of the fellow who took me away the night I was born. It took a deal of work, but eventually it was established that I was taken to an orphanage in Dublin, and adopted by William Jones.

'I felt some kinship with Barry even before he told me. He struck up a friendship with me, you know. We used to go out a bit together in Dublin. He professed an interest in my art, said I should go to England and set up a studio. Then when he told me the whole, we both got serious about it.'

'Why did you decide to become Count Borsini?' I asked.

'That was Margaret's idea. She said I had noble blood, and would have better luck in my career if I claimed a title. That meant being a foreigner. I could not claim to be a Frenchie, since

I cannot parlay the bongjaw well enough. Very few Englishmen speak Italian, so I became Count Borsini. I remember the night we chose the name. Barry and I were having a bottle of wine in the rooms I hired in Brighton. It was from the Borsini vineyards, so we decided I would be a younger son of Count Borsini.'

'And you made the mistake of putting those vineyards in Venice,' I reminded him.

'Ah, you remember that *faux pas*. I was hoping you had not noticed it.'

'Did you never plan to tell us who you are, Andrew?' I asked. 'When both Barry and Margaret were dead, surely there was no reason to keep quiet.'

'I have wanted to tell you for ever, but I could not find the marriage certificate. Without that, I felt very little claim on your friendship – a mere by-blow. You would be ashamed of me. I hoped that setting up your studio might provide an excuse to search Barry's room. I knew he had the document, for he showed it to us once at Lindfield. Margaret was touched that he had kept it all those years. Then yesterday Steptoe got in touch with me. He had seen me in Lindfield. The scoundrel had been spying through Barry's belongings when Barry was still alive, and saw the marriage license. Barry interrupted him before he had time to read the bride's name. Steptoe has been searching for it ever since, but he could not find it.

'He knew Barry met me in Tunbridge when he was supposed to be in London. He never spotted Margaret. She kept pretty close to the house. I don't believe Steptoe ever figured out what was going on. Being a thief himself, he suspected only financial chicanery, but there was nothing illegal in Barry selling the jewelry he brought home from India. A fine emerald necklace, a sapphire ring, a few other pieces. Margaret sold the diamond necklace herself, and claimed it was stolen, to avoid questions. Barry dealt with a different jeweler.'

I missed a golden opportunity to hold my tongue and said, 'Mr Bradford, at the Kashmir Jewelry Shop.' Weylin gave me a questioning look, but Andrew spoke on.

'That is right. I see you have been investigating, Cousin. Margaret and Barry wanted to see me comfortable in the world. They preferred to arrange all the transfers by cash, to be rid of the complications of a Will, which was bound to cause trouble. I did not urge them to do it. Money is not important to me. I don't need much, though I daresay I shall set myself up in a little higher style now that you folks are acknowledging me. Anyhow, I agreed to pay Steptoe a hundred pounds if he could find the marriage license.'

'I wonder why Steptoe left without finding it,' I said. 'It is unlike him to walk away from a hundred pounds. He must have assumed Barry destroyed it.'

'I wager he did not leave empty-handed,' Weylin said.

'He did not take the silver or any jewelry at least.'

A little later, Mary came bobbing into the saloon to say Mama was arranging the blue room for Mr Jones, and did I know what happened to the little blue and white jug that used to sit on the bureau. It was gone.

'No, I have not seen it, Mary.' Saint Brodagan has a heavy hand. In her new state of grace, she would no doubt confess to having broken it, if asked nicely. I said to Weylin, 'That is the little jug like the Ming vase you thought I was trying to steal at Parham. I mentioned it to you.'

'Ah yes, the Ming vase made in Italy.' Then his smile stretched to a wicked grin. 'Steptoe! *That* is what he ran off with! He mistook it for a genuine Ming. I knew he had not gone empty-handed. He will he disappointed when he tries to hawk it.'

Borsini – I must remember to call him Andrew – was smiling softly. 'Preparing a guest room for me?' he asked. 'Then she is willing to acknowledge me?'

'Willing and eager, even though she is unaware of that wedding document,' I assured him. 'She has bought sateen for new curtains for your room.'

'You will have uphill work trying to pry Andrew loose from Mama,' Weylin warned. 'He is a prime favorite there, too.'

Mama soon joined us, and the story was gone over again. She was completely enthralled with her new nephew.

'I always felt there was something in Borsini did I not say so, Zoie? I always felt – but it was those "*signoras*" that put me off a little. You must call me Aunt Flo, Andrew. Come and tell me if you like the blue room, or if you would prefer your papa's octagonal tower. Zoie can have her studio in another room.'

Knowing my keen interest in my studio, Andrew said at once that blue was his favorite color. I heard him assuring Mama as they went toward the staircase that he was never comfortable in an odd-shaped room.

'It seems we have found a new cousin, Weylin,' I said. 'How did your mama take the news?'

'Mama was as nearly happy as I have ever seen her. Also Bubbums. He is broadening his snacks to include paintbrushes. Mama was not so surprised as you may think. She always thought there was some mystery to Margaret's hasty marriage to MacIntosh. At the time of the so-called miscarriage, she began remembering a little gain in weight before the wedding, and what was called at the time a nervous stomach. But ladies, you know, did not discuss such things. Andrew is to be a cousin from Ireland, as we do not wish to jeopardize his inheritance by broadcasting the bigamous nature of Margaret's marriage. Morally the money is Andrew's. That is good enough for me.'

'It was kind of him to pretend he did not want my studio, was it not? He knows how much it means to me.'

'It is a shame a fine painter like Andrew does not have a studio, though. We have a nice, bright corner room at Parham that would take very little work to convert to a studio.'

'Weylin! You are not going to steal him from us entirely! We found him first!'

He rose and sat on the sofa beside me. 'You misunderstand me, Zoie. The corner room at Parham would make a fine studio for you.' A lazy light danced in his eyes, and his lips moved uncertainly.

Until he made his intentions clearer, I was obliged to misunderstand him. 'It would be inconvenient for me to have my studio at Parham and live here. Much better to have it where one lives.'

His arm moved along the sofa, to dangle over my shoulder. 'True. I daresay we could find you a bedroom as well, move you in bag and baggage. The only little difficulty is that you would have to share the bedchamber with me.'

'Are you not afraid I would make off with your Chinese porcelains?'

'What is mine is milady's,' he murmured, placing his hand on my shoulder and turning me to face him. 'My vases, my home, my name . . .'

The words blurred to a hum as his lips seized mine. I closed my eyes as his arms folded around me, crushing me to him. I was overcome again by the magic of the moonlit garden. A strange confusion of emotions whirled through my brain. It was all mixed up with Andrew and the sad tale of Barry and Margaret, and with leaving Mama to begin a new life at Parham. How could Margaret have let the man she loved sail away from her? My heart swelled within me, filling me with an unknown rapture, which must have been love. I knew I would follow Weylin to the ends of the earth, if that was what he wanted.

We did not hear Brodagan come in. She can move quietly when she wants to. The first intimation that we had company was a discreet cough. We flew apart in guilty haste, to see her staring at us. With her misshapen jaw, it was impossible to know whether she was smiling or frowning.

'Brodagan, you should be in bed!' I exclaimed.

'So should you, from the way the pair of you are carrying on,' she replied. 'Them chits from Parham can go home now, your lordship. I don't need any help but my Mary and Jamie. I'll not let an aching jaw detour me from my duties to my ladies.'

Weylin, awake on all suits, knew the way to cozen her. 'I wish you will let them stay a few days, Brodagan. They do not get the sort of training they need at Parham. It takes a masterful woman like you to trim the chits into line. You had best go and see they are not moping over a cup of tea. You know what servants are.'

'Aye, when the cat's away, the mice will play. As soon as melady comes down, I'll get a collar on your chits, melord.' She stood straight as a door, glaring at us until we drew a few inches apart. 'Well,' she said impatiently. 'Do you have something to tell me?'

Weylin said, 'You may be the first to congratulate us, Brodagan.'

A smile split her swollen face. 'My soul from the devil! You've nabbed yourself a fine lord, missie. And not a drop too good for you either,' she added to Weylin. 'So it is to be the middle-aisle jig. That's all right then. I'll leave you to it, but mind you don't let your joy get the better of you.'

She left with a swish of starched aprons, her steeple wobbling uncertainly.

'Quick thinking, Weylin,' I complimented.

'I have not been a politician all these years for nothing. I know when a colleague must be appeased. You will miss Brodagan.'

190

'Yes, like Brodagan will miss Mr Snaggle Tooth. If you are not hard enough on me at Parham, I can always come and visit her, to receive a scold.'

We settled in comfortably. Weylin said, 'What was that you mentioned to Andrew about a Mr Bradford, and a Kashmir Jewelry Shop? You did not tell me about him, when we were sharing our disgrace at Tunbridge.'

'You gentlemen have to learn the art of politics. Ladies are born possessing it.' I confessed all my little lapses, while he was still in the first throes of being engaged. His arm was around my shoulder, his fingers playing with my hair.

When I had confessed all, he said, 'You will make an admirable Whig hostess, my dear. The very soul of discretion. That is French for crooked as a dog's hind leg.'

'Thank you, sir. Now, to change the subject, it is the copy of the diamond necklace that first brought us together, and we *still* don't know what Barry was doing with it.'

'Andrew explained that to me. Barry had a copy made when Margaret decided to sell the original. She planned to wear the paste necklace, to conceal having sold the original. She was not happy with the copy, and said the necklace was stolen instead. Barry just tossed the copy in a drawer and forgot about it. And I, for one, am very happy he did, or I would never have got to know your delightfully warped character.'

'I am happy, too, for us and Andrew. It has taken a quarter of a century for the tale to reach this satisfactory conclusion. Three lives have been impoverished by Margaret's betrayal.'

'Let it be a lesson for us. I don't know how they could have hidden their joy from the world when they fell in love and married. Folks say love and a cough cannot be hidden. I can only conclude they did not love as *we* love, Zoie. I feel like hiring a platform and announcing our wedding to the whole parish.'

'An advertisement in the journals will serve the purpose,' I said, but truly I felt the same as Weylin. 'You need not hire a platform, but when I give you our first son, I want fireworks at Parham.'

His fingers tilted my face to his. 'There will be fireworks at Parham long before that, my dear, if *I* have anything to say about it.'